Letting the dice decide

A collection of short stories
~Halloween edition~

Letting the dice decide

A collection of short stories
~Halloween edition~
By Cara Solveig

Contents

Content warning

The following stories can contain mentions of dark topics like child negligence, murder of a child, kidnappings, and other topics readers might find triggering.

Read at your own risk.
Not suitable for anyone under the age of 16

Dedication

*To any and everyone who loves the creatures that go bump in
the night.*

Dracula – Spider's web – Witch's boot – Stary night

The owl hooted in the distance.

Dracula heaved a sigh. Having to clean the attic had not been his plan when he woke up this evening. He had hoped he could go out and cause a little terror and maybe a little mischief since it was Halloween night.

The only night of the year when people didn't run from him, screaming, when they saw him. He had got ready to go out and then he'd noticed something missing.

He couldn't find his favourite cape. The missing cape had spurred the impromptu clean-up. He couldn't remember when he'd last used his cape, but he couldn't exactly go outside dressed as himself without his signature cape, now could he?

Dracula moved a couple of boxes to the side he had already looked through and looked out the small window in the attic. He could barely see the moon, but he knew it was there. Dracula could see a few stars from the Orion constellation, despite the light pollution from the village below the hill. He had always hated the lights the people used at night. It ruined his view from the top of the hill, and he used to enjoy the view before the humans started hanging lights everywhere during the winter months.

Dracula picked up another box and looked through it. The cape wasn't there either.

Setting the box down harder than he had planned, set off a thick dust cloud that had Dracula coughing and stepping back to get away from it. Waving his hands in the air to disperse the cloud, he fumbled around, almost blinded by the dust particles.

He felt something sticky and strong on his face as he reached the corner of the attic. The spider's web had been empty, but the sticky substance still clung to his face.

Could this day get any worse?

He felt the box by his feet seconds before he tripped over it. He had tried wiping the web off of his skin with his sleeve as he had tried to get to the trapdoor, but his temporary blindness had caused him to miss the box on the floor.

Dracula landed on the floor with a loud oomph. He should have known better. It always got worse when a person said it couldn't.

He wiped at his face again with his sleeve, getting the rest of the spider's web off. He opened his eyes. His vision was blurry from the dust and the tears. He used his other sleeve to wipe at his eyes. Finding the red smear of his tears mixed with the spider's silk.

When he was finally comfortable opening his eyes again, he met the many eyes of the spider.

"I'm sorry. I didn't see your home there." Dracula muttered. The spider looked as if it huffed before crawling down from Dracula's sleeve.

He sighed deeply again. He should have done a more thorough job of cleaning the attic earlier in the year. Then he could have taken his time with it and not felt rushed because he wanted to go out.

Laying down on the dusty floor, he wanted to give up. Where could the cape be? Looking up at the inside of the tile roof, he thought about the entire situation. Should he just forget about going out and then hire someone to clean the attic once and for all? Hiring cleaning services wouldn't even put a dent in his wealth anyway – but did he want a stranger to go through his stuff while he slept? No, he'd better do it himself.

Dracula turned his head and saw something he didn't expect to see. He saw a boot that couldn't be his own. Not only didn't he own boots, but he could see from a distance it wasn't even his size. He only owned dress shoes.

Dracula got up and picked up the boot. He looked it over. It was smaller than his size and clearly a woman's boot.

He looked all over to figure out whom the boot belonged to. But he simply hadn't any idea who had left it in his attic. The place where he didn't entertain guests and where they would have had to lower the ladder and open the trapdoor to get to. He couldn't find the other boot, either.

Looking inside the boot gave him a clue. He only knew one person who wore boots of that brand. He put the boot under his arm and made sure it was secure by pressing his arm close to his body.

Dracula walked to the trapdoor and down the ladder to the floor. He went down all the flights of stairs from the attic to the ground floor. He had counted them at some point, and he knew there were 85 steps, which didn't sound like much, but when he was tired from flying, he didn't want to go down five flights of stairs to get to his coffin.

Getting to the ground floor, he reached into the hall closet and took one of his cloaks at random. The one he got out was dark grey from too many washings and the hem had frayed from too much use.

He didn't care now. He had to deliver the boot back to their owner, and then he needed to ask her what she had been doing in his attic.

Dracula walked out of the giant front doors and closed them behind him. He didn't care about locking them, because no one was foolish enough to try breaking into his home, and if they did, kudos to them.

Tugging the boot under his arm, he set out to find the owner. He had a feeling he'd find her in her home out in the forest, but he also knew he had to cross the entire town to get to the forest.

Deciding to go the scenic route and deciding against flying because the boot would be too heavy for his bat self, Dracula walked down the hill to the town. He hoped he would get to see some children in their Halloween costumes, but at the same time, he was sad that he couldn't get to take part like he usually did.

Dracula wanted to be in the celebration, the only day of the year when people didn't run away in fear from him. He'd hoped to spread a little good-natured terror amongst the adults and get some children to do some mischief.

Telling the children to go home and find all the toilet paper they could and then TP the garden of the local priest, or maybe even the church. He'd had ambitions this year, and it was all ruined now because of his favourite cloak going missing and now he had to deliver the boot back to the witch.

"Maybe she can tell me where my cloak is." He
wondered out loud. It was an option. The witch had
always been good at finding stuff, which made him
wonder again how and why her boot had been in his
attic. Had she placed it there on purpose?
A couple of children ran past him, not even sparing
him a glance. They were too busy going to the next
house to get more candy.
Dracula knew, from listening to parents complain the
day after Halloween, that the children always ate too
much candy and ended up with stomach aches the
day after.
He smiled at the thought. Even if he couldn't go out
and cause a little mischief, then the parents would still
have a mess to clean up, just a different one.
Walking past several more houses and several
children dressed as everything ranging from a copy of
himself to occupations their parents had. The longing
of being there himself lay heavy in his chest once
again. Whispering to the impressionable children what
they could do for tricks if they didn't get treats.
He walked past parents calling out to their children
that it was time to go home. Telling them that even
little monsters had bedtimes. If only they knew how
long monsters really stayed up at night.
Dracula sighed. He had to deliver the boot and then
he had to go back and finish searching for his cloak.
His absolute best cloak.
Trying not to ruin his own mood further, he started
walking faster. The faster he could get there and back,
the faster he might find his cloak and get back
outside. He hoped might be able to catch some of the
teenagers without bedtimes and talk them into
pranking the priest, at the very least.

Dracula got to the witch's house only ten minutes later. He lifted his hand to knock, but stopped himself when he noticed the door was already open.

Dracula had visited her before and knew he could go inside without trouble, and yet he stood there for a second to listen for the witch inside. Was she home or had something happened?

He heard her muttering words in Latin and decided just to walk in. She rarely did anything truly dangerous, and he was, after all, almost immortal.

The cauldron bubbled as it simmered on the fire in the middle of the room. The witch had decorated her little cabin with as many fire hazards as she could, but nothing ever caught fire that wasn't supposed to. At least, as far as Dracula knew.

There were massive tomes on shelves. The shelves looked like they were holding on for dear life, bowing down in the middle from the weight. There were piles upon piles of books on tables and paper sticking out from almost every surface imaginable.

She had small bottles with coloured substances, some of them glowing gently even in the darkness. Dracula couldn't tell if the substances could light up by themselves or if they glowed in the dark like some stars that children sometimes hung in their rooms. Dracula smiled at the sight. It seemed like he wasn't the only one with a wardrobe malfunction.

The witch had dressed like a true stereotype. She had striped stockings going half up her calves, one in green and black and the other in orange and black. She was only wearing one boot, matching the one Dracula had found in his attic.

The skirt she wore was loose and flowy with a tattered hem. The black colour had faded slightly and had spots of potions splattered on the fabric.
Her shirt was long-sleeved and black. The sleeves were bell-shaped and the bottom of them almost touched the potion in her cauldron as she stirred. There was powdered residue on her shirt that Dracula didn't even want to try identifying. The shirt hadn't faded as much as the skirt. It was clear she had just picked the first skirt and shirt in her closet.
Dracula chuckled. At least he wasn't the only one where things didn't go the right way this year. He wondered what she was mixing up in the cauldron. At the same time, it could be anything, so he didn't want to ask.
The witch looked up with a huge smile on her lips. "Dracula, how splendid to see you. I didn't expect you today." She said, her bubbling personality shining through her voice.
"I hadn't planned to come by either. The door was open, and you forgot something at mine's," Dracula said and held out the boot for her to see.
"Ooooh, splendid!" The witch let go of her giant spoon, which kept stirring in the cauldron. She clapped her hands together and went around the cauldron to take the boot from Dracula.
"Splendid?" Dracula asked. How could it be splendid that she had left her boot in his attic? Why had she been there in the first place?
"Why yes, splendid." The Witch smiled and gestured at the cauldron.
"See, I was testing out a transportation potion. I figured that if the boot got lost on the way, then it

wouldn't matter much. At least it wasn't me who got lost." She bent down to pull on the boot again.
"Can you imagine being stuck in an in-between place?" Her laughter sounded like bells jingling. She straightened after lacing up her boot.
"Ah, yes. I see." Dracula's smile didn't look all too genuine. Had he walked all the way there only to figure out she'd sent the boot there on purpose?
"Were you aiming for my attic?" Dracula asked. He needed to know for his own peace of mind. He wouldn't appreciate more of her things showing up in his already messy attic.
"Oh no, no. I didn't know where it would go. That's the joy of experimenting." The joyful glee almost bursting through her words.
"I suppose. I would appreciate no more sudden appearances in my home…" He said and turned to walk out of the witch's home.
"Did you check your closet?" The witch asked with a knowing smile.
Dracula looked back at her, his jaw dropping to the floor. He had checked the closet; he was sure.
Dracula nodded, and she shrugged.
"Maybe you should check again." She suggested with another kind smile, still stirring the cauldron in front of her.
Dracula just nodded, too dumbfounded to realise he had only looked at the rack of clothes and not truly searched in the closet.
The witch waved at him as he turned to walk out of her little cottage.
"Thank you." He whispered and left the little house. He walked back the same way he had walked earlier, trying to find the witch.

Getting home a lot later than he had planned, he went directly to the basement. Dracula went directly to his closet, just to prove the witch wrong.

He looked at each hanger, seeing only his dress trousers, his formal button-downs, and his dress shirts. Until he found an empty hanger.

Could it have fallen down?

He tried to look at the bottom of the closet, and sure enough, there it was.

Dracula picked up his favourite cape off the bottom of the closet and held it in his hands. He stared at it for a second before letting out a frustrated groan.

He could have spared himself the trouble of the attic cleaning and gone out.

Putting the cape back on the hanger, he stumped to his coffin. He was done.

Creepy eye – Witch's hat – Bat – Candle

The creepy eye on the top shelf was staring at me. I could feel it. Even though my best friend and coven sister had assured me it wasn't sentient or even truly seeing, it still felt as if it was staring at me all the time.

It was in a jar, floating in some kind of solution I didn't want to know the recipe for. I didn't have any idea why she had it in her possession to begin with. I had never come across any recipe which would use it. I'd never thought of asking her, but I might have to. Maybe, if it wasn't all that important for our craft, or some expensive artefact, then she could get rid of it.

I picked up the few containers of dried herbs I'd used for the talismans I'd been making. I was just a newbie at the craft, and I'd only just come into my powers. It had been a shock for me and for my family, when suddenly things started happening around me. Things I couldn't explain or stop from happening.

I'd been found by a coven leader who was my now best friend, and she began training me.

I say she's my coven sister, but in reality, I'm not in a coven yet. I want to be, but I need to fully develop my powers first.

So, I'm making talismans for my best friend, to see if that is the way I can channel my powers in the best way. I know it might not sound all that fun or interesting, but it is for me.

There's so much to learn and so many combinations possible, either with crystals or herbs or both, for the effect of the talisman to be different.

I had to study and what better way than to visit my best friend and use her books and herbs? A few of the herbs spilled in the process of being measured for the talismans, and I had to dust them all up.

I stood and put the containers back in their right spots, making sure I didn't mess up my best friend's system while sorting.

I eyed the jar with the eye inside, wondering if something bad would happen if I turned the jar around so the eye wasn't staring at me the way it was. Reaching up, I had to stand on my toes to even touch the bottom of the glass jar. I tried to move my fingers, so the glass turned around.

It took a few tries before the glass had turned and the eye was facing the wall.

Feeling a little better, I went back to the mess I'd made. I picked up the talisman, which was a little glass jar with a few herbs inside, and looked at it. It didn't look like much, but if done properly, it could be intense and too powerful for a newbie like me. I put it in my pocket, thinking I'd have to show my best friend my work when she came back.

I picked up the open book off of the floor and closed it. Putting it back on the bookshelf, I couldn't put it off anymore. I had to gather up the dried herbs.

I sat down on the floor, wondering about the best way to do it. Vacuuming it was an option, but I wasn't sure where she kept the vacuum cleaner. I could dust it up, but the dustpan had a lot of other mistakes on it, and I didn't know if mixing those would be safe. Bending down, I looked at the amount on the floor, realising that it wasn't as much as I had first thought. Maybe I could just blow it away?

Yep, that was what I was going to do. I leaned down with my head close to the floor and blew at the herbs. They scattered all over the floor, becoming less visible.

I sat up, pretty satisfied at my attempt at clean-up when smoke started gathering, like the type of thick fog one could usually see in the early hours of the morning at the beginning of autumn.

The type of fog that rolled in and hid anything close to the ground. I didn't know where it was coming from, but it was gathering above the herbs I'd just scattered.

What had I done?

Dread filled me and froze me in my tracks. *What exactly was happening?* I hadn't been playing with anything dangerous; I knew that much, and I couldn't possibly have done anything when I was mixing the herbs. Retracing my steps in my head, I tried to figure out just what I'd done wrong. I hadn't even spoken any words of invocation.

I had checked to make sure I could mix them for a talisman. It couldn't be that. It just couldn't.

The fog or smoke, or whatever it was, kept gathering on the floor, growing in size and darkness. *What else had I done that could have caused this to happen?*

Oh…

I'd been right…

Something was wrong with the jar and the eye, and I'd caused this when I'd turned the jar around. I cast a quick glance up at the jar, not wanting to take my eyes off of the smoke cloud gathering.

The eye had turned around and was staring at me again. I had to focus on the smoke. I had to get it out of the house before my friend got back home. I ran to the nearest window and tried to open it.

It was stuck in the corner, but I kept pushing on it until it gave way.

The breeze coming from the window was like a balm on my skin. I hadn't noticed how hot it had got inside the room before the outside air touched my skin.

The smell of brimstone and sulphur spread through the air, almost making me gag. I stayed by the window, trying to breathe in the clean air from the outside.

It didn't work.

Giving up on the fresh air, I looked back at the smoke. It hadn't moved; the breeze coming in from the window didn't even stir it a little.

The smoke started changing shape. Growing upwards, filling out the space. A dark shape appeared in the smoke, just an outline at first, with no real clear image, until it moved.

The monstrous shape stepped out of the smoke. It was like a creature from my worst nightmares. The skin was deep red, almost like blood. The size of the beast was a lot taller than me, and I had to look up to look at its head.

The creature had horns that curved upwards. They were even darker than the monster's skin colour. The wings were massive, and I had a fleeting thought for my best friend's casting room.

If I got rid of the creature, I'd have a hell of a clean-up to do. I hoped I'd be able to get rid of the monster before she got back.

The monster took another step forward, looking down at the floor. It stopped, or maybe I should say, he stopped. It was distinctly a male creature.

He looked up and gazed directly into my eyes with his violet ones. There were no mistakes. His eyes were violet, and it made his eyes stand out even more against the red of his skin.

"Really? No protective circle?" He smiled viciously, sending a chill down my spine. "Now, little witch, have you learned nothing?" He moved faster than I could perceive. I felt the wall behind me and his hot skin in front of me.

"Any dark witch worth their salt would know that a protective circle is a bare minimum when dealing with a demon…" He tsked at me. My entire being was on high alert. He was a demon. I'd made a demon appear, and I hadn't protected myself.

I wanted to flee, but hadn't any idea where to go. He was massive, and I had no way of getting around him. His dark, leathery wings closed me in and let very little light inside.

"A…a demon?" Had I just summoned a demon without meaning to? *No, this couldn't be happening!* How was I to get rid of a demon when I couldn't even make a bloody talisman without spilling herbs all over?

"Yes." His deep voice sounded like a growl to my ears and the chill down my spine intensified, making a stark contrast to the heat he was bathing me in.

"I'm Nymgarraman, servant of the infernal king Bilet, but you little witch…" He breathed very close to my hair. It was as if he was trying to inhale my entire being in one breath.

He was so close I could feel him vibrate with what sounded like a purr coming from his chest.

"You, little witch, can call me Nym." Nym gave no reason for my special privileges. He just gave me the nickname as if it was a reason for me to actually know it.

"I…" I started. I hadn't any idea what to say to that. Why would a demon give me a nickname to call him? I wanted to get him to leave and go back to where he came from.

"See now, I've been watching you, little witch." The gruff, gravelly voice had me pressing myself into the wall behind me to get away from him.

"W-why…?" I asked tentatively. If he was talking, maybe he wouldn't kill me. Maybe my best friend could come home, and she'd have a way to send the demon back or could go get help.

"Someone doesn't like you… They sent me to cause you great pain and suffering…" He let his words trail off, knowing exactly what effect they were having on me. Dizziness hit me as the blood drained from my head and if he hadn't been standing in front of me, keeping me up, I'm sure my legs would have given out already.

"I could make your limbs tremble, and it wouldn't even be painful." He mused with laughter in his voice. If I could, I wanted to meld into the wall to get away from him.

"You summoned me after all, little witch. Now, do you want me to punish someone?" He lifted a finger to my cheek and the heat from his skin radiated deep into me.

Who wanted to hurt me? Why hadn't Nym done it yet? Why did he seem to think I had summoned him? Would I want to hurt the person who wanted to hurt me?

"I… I didn't summon you…" I try to stop my voice from shaking, but I'm unsuccessful and the demon notices. He leans in, his face as close as he could be without touching me.

"Now, little witch, don't feel scared. I've yet to hurt you." He kept his eyes on me, pressing his hips against my middle.

"I don't want you to hurt me…" How was I going to get rid of him? Had I read about demons anywhere, or had any of the witches I knew told me about them? How did I banish him?

"How about we make a deal, little witch, hm?" He licked his lips. I couldn't see it, but I could feel it. The tip of his tongue accidentally touched my lower lip. I wanted to turn my head away from him, but I didn't want to expose my neck to him.

"What kind of deal?" I knew it was a bad idea to make deals with demons and I wouldn't ever do it, but maybe I could gain extra time to find a way of getting rid of him if I played along.

"We could say that I won't hurt you, and you come back to my home with me?" His sly smile told me enough of what he could do to me if he brought me back to his home.

I stared into his eyes, trying to come up with a counteroffer that wouldn't have me as a captive in the underworld, or wherever he came from.

"No…" He tsked at me, the sound loud enough to make me flinch.

"So, you want to get hurt, kinky…" He chuckled and leaned in further to scent me again. He could probably smell the fear on me, and he seemed to enjoy it a little too much. His clawed hand touched my cheek, almost gently, but I wasn't fooled. I knew he was strong enough that he could snap my neck if he wanted. He probably didn't even need to touch me to do it.

"Now, kinky little witch, I could promise to hurt you, just a little, but not kill you…" He stated, looking almost bored. I could see the emotions floating around in his violet eyes. He was anything but bored. His expression turned amused, and it looked like he knew he'd be getting what he wanted, one way or another.

"In exchange for what?" I asked. I didn't want him to hurt me, but if the option was getting hurt by him or getting killed, I'd choose the latter.

"In exchange for coming back with me, I could give you the world before I take your soul and your body. I'm sure you'd like that part…" He pressed closer to me, making sure I couldn't get away. His massive size almost crushed me, even as he was leaning down towards me to meet my eyes.

"Don't demons just want souls in their deals?" I had to ask. I knew that if one made a deal with the devil, they'd forfeit their soul. Wasn't dealing with demons the same?

"Usually, yes, but witches are interesting playthings, and life in the demon-realm can get a little dull." He wasn't telling the entire truth, and I could tell. I hadn't any idea why he really wanted me to go with him in exchange for not hurting me.

I crept my hands up, wanting to surprise him with a push or some magic or anything, really. Desperation was getting the better of me. I wasn't thinking clearly. I could feel the talisman in my pocket, and slowly I edged my hand inside my pocket to take it out. Maybe I could use it. The herbs inside probably wouldn't do anything against him, but it was worth a try.

The worst he could do was kill me, so I'd rather go down fighting. He hadn't hurt me yet and maybe he wouldn't at all.

I opened the talisman and then pushed it at his chest. He roared and stepped back a few steps. His eyes swirled with anger and malice. He lifted a hand towards me, but before he would do anything against him, he disappeared.

Behind where he'd been stood my best friend, with an outstretched hand. The smell of brimstone still hung heavy in the air, worse now that the demon was gone again.

"What's that on your cheek?" My best friend asked, horrified from the doorway. I hadn't any idea what was on my cheek, and it didn't matter. I didn't question why she didn't ask about the demon she'd just helped me get rid of. I was just happy that it was gone and there were more important things to take care of.

Standing in the middle of the mess the demon had left behind, I looked up at my best friend.

"That creepy eye has got to go!"

3

Creepy Eye – Ghost – Witch's hat – Weird one-eyed monster

Caught in a fairy ring.
I was bloody caught in a fairy ring! The thoughts whirled around my mind. How did I get so careless that I got caught in a fairy ring?
I crouched down and leaned my head close to the edge of the ring to examine it further. Hidden well in the grass was the tiniest line of little mushrooms. An unbroken line, the sign of a true and working fairy ring.
Sighing deeply, I sat down on the wet grass. It would take ages for someone to find me and then it would take them ages to find something made of iron to disrupt the fairy ring with.
There was no other way around it - I was doomed to stay in the fairy ring. It was as simple as that.
Doomed. I picked up my hat, which had fallen off when I'd walked into the barrier, closing me in. I dusted it off gently. *Why couldn't I have been paying more attention?*
I had just been visiting my coven leader to see some new potion ingredients that she had found. She had preserved a big creepy eye in vinegar to show me as a new potion ingredient.

The eye would do well in a potion for looking into the future or seeing through things. I was sure of it. She had been nice enough to give me the glass, and I'd been looking at the eye instead of looking at the ground.

I was so stupid.

I looked around and found the glass on the ground, outside of the fairy ring.

Oh, no! My coven leader would kill me if I lost it. I have lost a thing or two through the years, but I'd got better. This just couldn't happen.

I began searching my pockets and my bag for anything I could use to remove the barrier, but I found nothing that wasn't made of wood or fabric. Nothing made of iron.

"No, no, no, no, this can't be happening," I mumbled - to no one in particular - like my words would function as a spell to remove my invisible prison.

I tried to search through my bag again, emptying everything out on the wet grass in front of me, but it was no use. How am I supposed to get out of here?

I knew of stories told about fairy rings, of how the person or people trapped had been trapped for hours or even days because time moves differently in the fae realm. A year for them might be a minute for us.

I'd heard of people being found dead in fairy rings. No one knows what had happened to them other than they looked like they had starved to death. I didn't want that to be my fate.

My heart was racing even as my chest tightened as desperation crawled up inside me. Claustrophobia had never been something I'd suffered from, but it crept up on me in the tight space of the ring. I had to get out of there. I didn't have anyone who would search for me in time.

"Help?!" I tried to yell, but only felt the sound reverberate back to me from the invisible barrier. No sound carried through. *Well, that was unfortunate*, but it made sense how people could have died in the rings without getting help. If no one had heard them scream.

A noise reached my ears, and I looked up. I couldn't see anyone. I looked behind me to each side, but I saw no one. Putting it down as wishful thinking. I continued to search through my things and put them back in my bag again. I still hadn't found anything made of iron.

The noise came again, and I wondered just how I could hear noises from outside my prison when my own words bounced back at me.

I supposed magic had its ways, but I really needed someone to hear me and get me out of there. Looking around at the grass around me, inside the circle, I made sure that I'd got everything back in my bag.

I ignored the sounds coming from the bushes, thinking it was the wind or a bird or a rabbit. It didn't sound like an enormous animal, and I felt somewhat safe inside the circle, even if I couldn't get out by myself.

A high-pitched whine had me looking up. What met my eyes had me screaming. The loud sound, thrown back at me, hurt my ears and I had to cover them to shield myself.

The monster standing outside of the circle was one of the horror stories my mother had told me as a child. It was a small one. It probably only came up to my knee if I was standing. The monster had one eye and a fuzzy bluish pelt. It didn't look like it had a mouth, and I hadn't any idea how it had made the whine. The monster was staring at me with one eye, and I didn't know if it would come into the circle or if it would leave me be when it found out I had trapped myself in here. It looked tense as it stared at me, and I stared back.

"Can you help me?" I tried to mouth the words to it, but it only bent its head and kept staring.

"Can you get me out?" I tried to enunciate the words properly in the hopes the monster would understand, but it just stood there. I tried pointing at the circle, but it didn't even follow my fingers or where they were pointing.

"Can you understand me?" I tried again, but it just stood still, staring at me. I didn't like it, not even a little. Not only was I looking at something that shouldn't exist, but I had also trapped myself with no way of getting away from it.

The monster walked around the circle on its little legs. It kicked any leaves and rocks away like it was making sure there was nothing within reach for me to help me out of the circle. It got to the glass with the weird eye inside it.

The monster bent down and picked the glass up and looked at the weird eye. It looked like it was tilting its head one way and the other to examine the glass and the contents inside it.

I rushed to the invisible wall of my cage, banging on the non-existent bars of my prison, trying to get the attention of the little monster, but it didn't even flinch at my banging. It turned its back to me and walked away, carrying the glass in its arms.

I slumped to the ground, feeling the tears brimming in my eyes. *This couldn't be happening.* Not only was I trapped, but I'd also lost the one thing I was supposed to keep safe.

"Please… someone help…?" I called out between soft sobs. I couldn't hold back the tears anymore. I felt so helpless, and I was afraid I was going to die in there.

"Please, Goddess, send someone to help me." I looked up at the sky, hoping that the deity could hear me despite the silencer placed on the fae ring prison.

"Please, I beg of you, Goddess. Help your daughter." I was sobbing earnestly now, with tears running down my cheeks and dragging whatever makeup I'd put on, this morning, down with them.

My eyes were stinging when I finally stopped crying and I didn't know how long I cried, or when I'd laid down on the ground, clutching my knees to my chest, but my tears had dried by the time I felt an icy presence near me.

I looked up, curious to see what was causing the icy feeling. What met my eyes was less scary than meeting the monster from earlier. The figure before me took the shape of a young man. It didn't look like someone I knew, but he looked kind.

The ghost hovered above the ground, its feet hazy and more transparent than the rest of him. It was as if the closer he got to the ground, the more transparent he got.

I looked at his head, trying to focus on the most tangible part of him. He looked like he was speaking, but I couldn't hear him. His lips were moving, but no sound passed through the barrier of the circle.

"I can't hear you…" I tried to say, knowing that the sound couldn't pass through from my side either. The ghost shook his head, showing that he couldn't hear me. He looked around our surroundings and then did something unexpected. He took a step and passed through the ring into the circle.

I stepped back, careful not to touch the invisible wall behind me. The ghost became even more transparent as he stepped through the circle, but regained some of the opacity when he was fully inside the circle with me.

I could feel my heart beating wildly in my chest and my breathing was shallow and fast. I had never been this close to a ghost before, let alone seen a ghost before.

It was a wild experience and if I hadn't been exhausted already, I might have freaked out a bit more about meeting a ghost for the first time. Especially one who seemed like he wanted to help me.

"Why are you here?" The ghost asked. I couldn't place the accent anywhere, but I understood his words, regardless.

"I wasn't looking…" I said simply, not wanting to explain just why I hadn't been looking at where I was going. The ghost just hummed and nodded his head, like it made sense for a witch to walk through a forest known for fairy rings, to not be looking at where she was walking.

"Can you help me get out?" I asked him and his face changed, turning sad. He shook his head from side to side, almost violently.

"I can't break the circle." He said. I didn't know if he couldn't break it because it was physically impossible for him to do so or if it was because he wasn't allowed to break it.

"Can you find someone for me to help me?" I asked instead. Hoping that maybe the ghost could find my coven leader and get her to bring iron to let me out. The ghost was about to shake its head again, but then stopped. It seemed like a lightbulb went off inside his head.

"Yes, yes, I can do that." He said, almost giddy with excitement that he could help me after all.

"Who do you need me to find?" He asked, almost jumping up and down on the spot, glee spreading on his face.

"I would really be happy if you could find my coven leader. She'll know what to do if you lead her here. Ask her to bring something iron." I said and hoped that the ghost could communicate with my coven leader the same way he could communicate with me. The ghost disappeared from my sight. He just vanished into thin air. I hoped he could find my coven leader even as I hadn't told him her name.

Once again, I was alone. I felt the wind pick up, and I looked up at the sky. The clouds were gathering and the smell of rain about to fall hit my nostrils. I hoped it would hold, but I was never that lucky.

Several minutes passed as I sat there in the fairy ring, hoping against hope that help would arrive soon.

I had almost given up on anyone finding me when I saw a soft light coming from the direction I'd been coming from. The strobe of light becoming brighter and brighter, closely followed by the ghost, floating smoothly through the air and my coven leader.

I stood and dusted off my clothes. I was done with being trapped and I just wanted to get out. The coven leader stepped closer and tried speaking to me, but I couldn't hear her. I shook my head and pointed at my ears.

She stopped talking and instead walked around the fairy ring to find a weak spot. The small mushrooms were almost making a double and very thick line in the grass now. It was like they had grown while I was trapped in their circle.

The coven leader furrowed her brows as she looked at them. I could just imagine her thinking that I couldn't possibly have missed a fairy ring with that many mushrooms.

I wanted to explain everything to her, and I wanted to tell her we needed to find the little monster and get the eye back, but I knew she wouldn't be able to hear me.

I had to wait patiently for her to break the circle and get me out, preferably before any of the fae would come and check who had been stupid enough to step into the circle.

The coven leader kept walking around in circles before deciding to find iron. She mouthed "This might hurt" to me and I tried to step into the middle of the circle.

She picked up a key made of iron out of her bag and neared it to the barrier. I braced myself. I'd never tried being caught in a fairy ring before, or seen anyone caught in one, so I didn't exactly know what happened when a circle broke.

The key touched the barrier, and it snapped with a loud crack. It sent a small shockwave of both the outside sounds and the magic breaking down.

I hadn't noticed how muted all the sounds of the forests had been before. I could only imagine just how loud the monster's whines had been.

"Thank you, thank you so much! I was afraid I'd have to stay there until the fae came to take me." I had fallen to the ground outside of the circle and sat there breathing heavily. The reality truly hit me at that moment. I could have spent all eternity in the fairy ring with no one the wiser.

"You should have been more careful. Didn't you watch where you were going?" My coven leader asked, and I lowered my head, properly chastised for my lack of attention. I'd learned my lesson, that's for sure!

"Looking at the glass you lent me had me preoccupied…" I excused myself and then stood.

"We need to catch that little monster who took the glass!" I exclaimed, making the coven leader almost jump at my sudden outburst.

"What do you mean? Don't you have it still?" The coven leader asked me. I could tell she was trying hard not to yell at me before she had the entire story. I didn't really want to tell it, but it was important so we could get the glass back.

"It fell out of my hands when I walked into the barrier. It fell to the ground outside of the fairy ring and then a monster came, stared at me, and then took the glass and walked away…" I explained and had already started walking in the same direction as I'd seen the monster take.

My coven leader walked right behind me, letting me lead. I felt a little touched that she would trust me to let me take care of at least one of my messes by myself.

I kept eying the ground, making sure I didn't step into another fairy ring. That could have been embarrassing.

We kept walking through the underbrush, keeping an eye out for signs that the little monster had gone this way. I tried to listen for its whines too, but I heard nothing.

We were walking in circles, but my coven leader didn't comment on it.

Suddenly the ghost from earlier showed up in front of me, silent as the grave with a cold, transparent finger in front of my lips. I stilled, staying completely silent, even as the ghost had surprised me.

The ghost turned and pointed off to the side. I raised a brow in question, and he just kept pointing. It was clear he wanted me to change directions, so I did.

I didn't know if the coven leader had seen the ghost in front of me or not, but she still followed behind me.

It only took us a few moments before we came upon the monster. It was sitting on a fallen tree, trying to open the mason jar. Why it was trying to do so, I hadn't any idea.

I crept up behind it and as quickly as I could; I snatched the glass out of its hands and held it up where it couldn't reach it.

The monster whined loudly, almost splitting my eardrums. My coven leader chose this time to come forward. She held some sort of powder in her hands. I couldn't tell what it was, but it looked like very fine salt.

"Go away…" my coven leader hissed at the monster before letting a bit of the salt fall from her hand onto the monster. The monster's skin sizzled, and then it popped out of existence.

"What did you do to it?" I asked, still holding the glass in my hands.

"Those kinds of fae don't like salt all that much. It didn't permanently harm it, but it'll know to not come back." My coven leader turned towards me and held out her hands for the glass.

"Now. I think I'll take this back. We can test out the magic when you come to visit." She said. I handed her the glass, feeling a bit dejected at the outcome of the night.

She smiled at me kindly and then began walking back towards her home. I stood there in the forest, just letting all the events sink in, and then I walked home. Careful of any fairy circles this time.

4

Skull – Ghost – Candle – Castle

"Come on! It'll be fun!"

Those words always prelude something horrible. It'll never be fun, it'll be absolutely horrible, and I knew my friends were down for it.

We had agreed to complete one of the oldest Halloween challenges in our town. It was one of the most cliché ones too, but many of our friends had already tried it and got scared. We wanted to be the ones to succeed.

We'd talked about doing the challenge for years, but had lacked the courage to do it, at least before this year. This year would be different. I had to make sure of it.

My best friend, Leonel, had spoken to our two other friends, Fox and Zev, about the challenge. We were trying to get them to go with us. *The more the merrier, right?*

They were hesitant, just like I had been at first, but I'd been convinced it was worth trying and so would they.

We'd agreed to meet outside of the haunted and empty castle as soon as the sun went down on the 31st of October. If we were going to do this, we would do it right.

We'd packed flashlights and extra batteries. We knew it was dark where we were going as the castle had been empty for a while now, according to the legends, and we didn't want to get caught in the basement .
"Okay, so the challenge is to go in there and find the skull of the old owner, right?" Fox asked, and we all just nodded. He put his hands in his pockets, shaking his long blonde bangs away from his eyes.
The dare, or the challenge, was several years old. For all we knew, the castle had been empty ever since we'd been born, and maybe even before that. We knew no one had dared to buy the house, and the rumours had existed even longer than we had been alive.
There were rumours that the old owner haunted the castle, and that was the most believable rumour out of the bunch. Some said the owner was a vampire and anyone who went inside to find the skull would end up as the vampire's dinner. That rumour had kept away most people.
We all knew that the last one was rubbish. We hadn't heard of anyone not surviving the dare, though no one wanted to talk about it.
I was sure it was that the failed attempt had embarrassed them because they couldn't finish the challenge and chickened out either before going in or before getting to the basement. In my book, it would be enough to just get past the front door.
I had to admit that looking up at the creepy old castle. My feet were getting colder by the minute. I didn't tell my friends. I didn't want to be known as the wuss in our group and since it had been me, and my best friend's idea to do this, I couldn't chicken out.

I pulled out my flashlight to check the batteries. I turned it on and shone the light on the huge door right in front of us. The bright and strong light made me feel a little safer. I knew I needed to save the batteries, so I turned off the flashlight again before we went in there.

"Are we all ready?" My blonde friend, Fox, asked and we all just nodded.

"Okay then. Let's go!" Fox smiled and charged ahead. He walked up to the door and pulled at the door handle. It wasn't really a door handle, but sort of like an iron ring that had to be pulled to open the door. It was heavy and Fox struggled with lifting it, but the door didn't budge for him, but he kept pulling.

"A little help here?" He looked accusingly over his shoulder. We all rushed to help him and finally, the door started moving and opening for us.

We opened the door enough for us to slip inside. The lack of light bathed the inside in darkness and shadow. There was light from the outside shining in, but it wasn't enough to see anything beyond those small spots by the windows.

We moved as a group through the hall. None of us had ever been in here before. We knew we had to go down and not up, but we needed to find the stairs first.

Zev and Leonel started turning on their flashlights, and their strobes of light illuminated a lot more than the moon did from the outside.

I didn't light mine, because I wanted to save some of the battery on it since we didn't know what could happen to us in this house. I kept it shut off as a safety precaution. The others didn't worry about not being able to see anything later.

The hallway didn't have any furniture, but was completely empty except for a dark rug on the floor. We moved into the next room, still not seeing any stairs that would lead down. White sheets covered each piece of furniture in the room. The castle was big, and no one had ever found blueprints or a map of the place. So, we went in blind, huddled close together and moving as one.

Since nothing showed up to scare us, we slowly drifted apart in the room, trying to find the location faster.

"Wouldn't it be fun if the skull was actually upstairs instead of in the basement? I mean, everybody who has searched for it, searched in the basement." I said. The thought of the basement sent chills down my spine. I felt safer if we were going upstairs instead of down.

"Have you ever heard of the prize of a dare being anywhere other than down in the crypt?" Leonel asked. He was searching through drawers on a desk. The white cloth that had covered the desk lay in a crumpled heap on the floor.

"No, but I've heard of treasure hidden in the attic," I answered him, hoping he'd take the bait. I'd more than happily fail the dare and say we tried, than end my life down in a dank crypt under a castle. No one would ever find our bodies here.

"There's a door over here?" Zev called out to the rest of us and we all went to him. The door was closed, and Zev reached out to open the door.

"Shouldn't we check the upstairs first?" I asked, trying to keep my voice confident. All three heads turned to look at me.

"Are you stupid or just a chicken?" Leonel asked incredulously. I winced. I didn't want them to know how scared I was.

"No. I just feel like the skull could be upstairs just as it could be in the crypt." I argued. "It would be the reason no one else has found it yet." It felt like I was just repeating myself and they weren't listening.

"No! It makes sense that it's down in the crypt. Where else would you hide a skull?" Fox said, and I put both hands up in defeat. They outnumbered me, and we were going to the crypt.

Going down the stairs, the steps creaked. I didn't like it. The darkness seemed to engulf us and I didn't like it, even with the flashlights. I turned my flashlight on, thinking this would be the time I would need it.

We walked down and kept walking. It felt like the stairs went on for miles when, in reality, it was only around 20 steps to get down to the basement.

It looked old and smelled very damp. I don't know if there was mould anywhere, but it didn't smell clean. Wrinkling my nose, I tried to ignore the smell and just look around the first room.

There wasn't much inside. There was a lot of old furniture, but that made sense considering how long ago it had been since someone lived here last. Some of the furniture had broken, and the owners hadn't thrown them out. The furniture down here weren't covered in sheets, but that only helped the creepy feeling along.

I figured the skull wouldn't be in the first room. Everybody who had been searching for it had searched the first room, or so they had told everybody who would listen. It couldn't be in here.

My friends seemed to agree with my unspoken thought and, as a group, we tiptoed into the next room through an open door.

One of the flashlights flickered. I didn't think much of it, but when the other started flickering, my heartbeat quickened. I just wanted this to be over. Zev, who was holding the flashlight, tried to bang it against his hand, to make it stop flickering, but it only made it worse. His flashlight went out completely.

"Did anyone bring extra batteries?" Zev asked, and all of us nodded. It seemed like he was the only one who hadn't brought any. I fished out the extra batteries I had, wanting to seem brave when, in reality, I was shaking in my pants.

He changed the batteries, and the flashlight again joined the other flashlights in illuminating the crypt. That only lasted for a few seconds before it flicked off again.

"Did you bring used batteries?" He accused me. I shook my head no. I'd brought them from the cupboard at home where my parents kept the new batteries. It had been a new packet of batteries I'd fished them out of.

"No, they were new…" I said, to back-up my head shaking. He huffed and then looked at the others. Fox's flashlights flicked off. We all looked at each other. We were down to two flashlights now. I didn't like the thought of that.

Fox found new batteries and changed them, throwing the old batteries on the ground. It happened again. This time, my flashlight went out with the other two. We were down to one flashlight and no more extra batteries.

"Do we turn around?" I asked. They all shook their
heads no. Leonel used his flashlight to look around
the room we were in. We noticed the torches on the
wall and thought that maybe those wouldn't just
flicker off as the flashlights had done.
"Did anyone bring matches?" I asked, looking at the
torches. Leonel's flashlight started flickering as well,
and like a ticking clock, we knew it was a sign that we
had to hurry. We all searched for matches in our
pockets and on the ground or near the torches.
"Here!" Fox yelled and held up a box of matches. We
lit one and tried to light the torch. It didn't work, and
the match went out right before it burned his fingers.
He lit another one, and that one seemed to do the
trick. The torch lit up with a burst of flame. He
picked it out of the holder on the wall and used it to
light around the room. It lit the room better than the
flashlights had done.
We looked around for more torches and found one
further ahead. We went to it and used the torch that
was already lit to light it. Leonel picked up the other
torch.
"Where do we go next?" Zev asked. We didn't answer
at first, we just looked around to find out where we
could go.
"How about that door?" Leonel pointed at a door in
the corner. We just shrugged and decided that any
door was better than no door. My best friend went
first. He opened the door, and we went through it.
A gust of wind came out of nowhere and blew out
the torches. Luckily, we hadn't got rid of the matches.
We huddled together in the dark to guard against the
wind.

Fox, who had the matches, lit one and tried to light
the torches. They both lit up easily. With a
triumphant smile, we all looked up to see what was in
the room.
What met us would haunt me forever. A translucent
shape of an old man was right in front of us, staring
at us with dead eyes.
We screamed. High-pitched and loud screams. The
torches dropped to the ground, going out again. We
all turned on our heels and ran.
Running as fast as our legs could carry us, we
screamed the entire way out of the castle. We didn't
wait for each other or stopped before we reached
home.

The screaming reverberated through the crypt. The
ghost looked over its shoulder at the throne-like seat.
"It's always the same, isn't it?" He said, and the man
sitting on the throne nodded.
"Yes, they never complete the dare. Any of them."
He said with a sad tone of voice.
"Such a shame, really. The skull is right here." He
held up the skull in his hand and a wicked grin on his
red lips.
"Yes, such a shame… Should we mix it up for next
year?" The ghost asked. The man's grin grew wider,
showing off the sharp incisors.
"Yes, we should."

Castle – Pumpkin – Broom – Skull

The skull sailed through the air, knocking the small statue off of the stone wall surrounding the property.

"Nice!" Eric yelled as Derek did a victory jump.

"Should we go get the skull again?" Derek asked, ready to go get it and try to hit something else.

"Nah, I'm sure there'll be more!" Eric said.

Their street didn't really celebrate Halloween by going trick or treating, but Erik and Derek enjoyed wreaking a little havoc under the guise of 'trick' in trick or treat.

They didn't want to dress up in costumes. They thought they were too old and, as the only people under the age of 16 on their street, they didn't see a need for it.

Their neighbours always decorated their houses and yards for Halloween, even if they didn't have bowls of candy out as most other people had at this time of the year, but there were plenty of pumpkins, skulls, ghosts, skeletons and so on.

The neighbours sometimes held decorating contests during the holidays, and Derek and Eric were sick of it. Everything had to look perfect. The decorations had to be just right, or the neighbours would gossip.

Derek had the idea to shake it up this time, and it didn't take long to convince Eric.

They decided that for this Halloween, everyone had to be equal. They would make sure that there'd be no winner for this year's contest. Instead, Derek and Eric would have fun tricking instead of treating.

They had planned sleepovers at each other's places and their parents didn't really care what they were doing. Eric's mom thought they were both at Derek's and Derek's mom thought they were both at Eric's, so they had plenty of time before any of their parents would wonder where they were. They had spent hours planning and they couldn't afford for their parents to ruin it.

"Let's go to the next house," Eric said and pointed at the neighbour's house. Derek just followed.

The house was one of the few with lights on it, and it was so tempting for them to hit the lights and smash them.

The boys walked up to the windows and looked inside. It didn't seem like anyone was home, so they felt a little safer in their plans.

Picking up a handful of small stones from the driveway, they started throwing stones at the lights.

"10!" Eric yelled as he moved around the house.

"Hah! I got 13!" Derek answered, moving the other way around the house with a handful of stones. Erik didn't answer, but Derek knew it was only because Eric wanted to win their minor battles. He was probably trying to smash more of the lights.

"There was a skeleton in the backyard, so I threw it into the enormous tree they have back there," Eric said as he came back around the house.

"Damn, nicely done!" Derek held his hand up, ready
to give Eric the high-five he thought he deserved.
"Next house?" Derek asked, and Eric just smiled and
nodded. This was more fun than sitting at home
watching the usual Halloween films they would show
on the television.
The next house had several carved pumpkins on the
front steps to their front door. Each carving was
more decorative and detailed than the next. Both boys
couldn't help but be a little impressed. The most
they'd ever been able to do was the usual eyes, nose,
and mouth with sharp teeth.
"Kick them?" Eric asked. Walking to the top of the
steps.
"Kick them!" Derek confirmed. Starting at the
bottom of the three steps. That it had probably taken
a while to carve the pumpkins didn't faze either of
them.
The pumpkins smashed completely when they landed
on the ground below the stairs, and Eric couldn't help
his smile growing wider. Next year, he'd convince his
parents to get a lot of pumpkins and then he'd carve
them, and then he'd throw them around the garden.
He would call it the pumpkin massacre.
"This is getting boring…" Eric said as they walked to
the next house on the street. This house had the same
type of decorations as the first house had. There were
bones scattered on the ground, along with piles of
dirt, looking like people were trying to dig their way
out of the ground.
"But we still have a lot of houses left to do," Derek
argued, but Eric just shook his head.

"We can do them afterwards. I want to go somewhere
else…" Eric said and started walking towards the
castle.

"Where do you have in mind?" Derek asked, trying to
keep up with Eric, who started walking before Derek
had been ready.

"Do you remember that big castle at the top of the
hill?" Eric asked, feeling emboldened by their tricking.
The castle would definitely have plenty of things they
could smash or break.

Having a creepy castle basically meant that the owner
had to decorate for Halloween. It was in the contract
- Eric was sure of it.

"Yes, I remember. Is that where you want to go?"
Derek liked the thought of going to the castle.

Usually, all the adults, even the teachers in school, had
told them all to keep away from the castle, saying that
the owner was crazy and the castle itself was full of
traps and dangers of all sorts. They both thought of
the stories as nothing but unconfirmed rumours.

A howl tore through the air, the sound both really
close and really far away from them.

"What was that?" Eric asked, not wanting to sound
scared, but still wanting to know what it had been.

"I'm sure it was just a dog. Either way, it was coming
from far away," Derek said, and lightly tapped Eric's
shoulder.

"Now, don't be a wuss. Let's go up there and check it
out. Who's going to stop us?" Derek started running
towards the hill in the distance, not waiting for Eric to
follow, but knowing he wouldn't be far behind.

Derek had to bend over, trying to catch his breath
when he got halfway up the hill. Laughing, Eric
passed him.

"Try to keep up, slowpoke," He yelled after Derek, who despite breathing heavily, started running again, not wanting Eric to win this time.

"So, do we just knock on the door and ask to go inside?" Derek asked, looking up at the imposing castle with the dark windows. There were gargoyle statues at the top, and the door was massive and made of oak. The rest of the castle were grey bricks and mortar. The entire building loomed over the both of them.

There were absolutely no Halloween decorations to be seen anywhere on the grounds in front of the castle or anything on the walls.

"Why haven't they decorated just a little?" Eric asked, wondering if he could turn them into the authorities and get them fined for not decorating for a national holiday.

"Maybe they don't like Halloween?" Derek suggested, feeling a little sad that their plan had been foiled. He was still breathing hard from all the running, but he was regaining control over his lungs.

"Who doesn't like Halloween?" Eric asked with disbelief clear on his face and in his tone of voice.

"We've just smashed several Halloween decorations ourselves. I think it's fair to say that some people might be tired of them?" Derek tried to argue, his breathing a little laboured still. Eric didn't like that Derek's words made sense. Why did they make sense?

"So, what do we do now? It doesn't seem like anybody's home?" Eric asked, feeling the urge to go up the steps and try the door. Derek looked around the grounds, locating a place they could hide.

"We could ring the doorbell and hide behind those big trees there…" He pointed towards their potential hiding place. "And then we can see if anyone's home?" he added. Eric nodded. He was closest to the door, so he skipped up the stairs and then rang the doorbell. He could hear it ring on the other side of the massive door before he started running for cover. They waited behind the trees for a little while, before realising that no one was there.

"Do we see if the door's unlocked and try to go inside?" Eric asked. He really wanted to go inside and look around. The place had been off-limits for so long that the temptation was nearly killing him. It wasn't just about ruining Halloween anymore, but the bragging rights for all eternity.

"Sure, we can try... but how about we make sure that no one is home?" He asked, looking around the grounds.

"And how do you suppose we do that? Ring the doorbell again?" Eric asked, not really sure what plans Derek had come up with.

Bending down to pick up a stone from the ground. He weighed it on his hands, judging it to not be heavy enough to break the glass, but big enough to make a noise that would have the owner come running.

"Wait here..." Derek said. Eric watched him go to the nearest window and throw the rock at the glass. The howl that followed the sound of breaking glass sounded so close that the only option was trying to get inside the castle to hide.

Eric started running and got to the door before Derek. Derek had frozen, staring at the broken glass, blood draining from his face. He hadn't wanted to break it.

Trying the handle, Eric opened the door easily, realising that it wasn't locked, to begin with.

"Hurry up!" Eric called to Derek, and it seemed to get Derek out of his frozen state. He started running towards the door as the third howl of the night broke through the night, sounding closer than ever.

Finally, inside, they closed the door behind them, trusting that whatever creature was out there hadn't learned how to open a door.

They looked around the entrance, amazed at how the castle felt homey on the inside. Wasn't it supposed to be a scary castle with traps and dangers? It didn't feel like it was. It felt like a normal home.

They heard something land on the floor in a room near the front door. The creature had got inside. They'd forgotten about the broken window.

Derek looked around for places they could go, but it was Eric who found a door. The growling started up, and they decided that regardless of what was behind the door, they'd go inside and hide.

Opening the door, they found wooden stairs that looked older than both of them combined. They walked down a few steps and closed the door behind them. The stairs creaked, and it felt like it could collapse at any moment.

They stood there listening for a little while, hoping the creature would walk past the door.

Eric tried to signal to Derek in the dark that they should try to go down and see what was in there, or if there were any light switches.

Feeling around on the wall beside the door, they found a switch and switched it on. A single lightbulb illuminated the stairs, but they could easily see at the bottom that it wasn't the only lightbulb down there. They decided that going down the stairs and checking for another way out was better than staying.

The growling behind them startled them and had them running down the stairs. Each step creaking more than the last. They hadn't any idea where the dog was, but they had a feeling it was rather large and scary and neither of them wanted to meet it face to face.

"In here!" Eric whispered, pointing at a giant cage in the basement room. They both hurried inside and pulled the cage door closed behind them.

They'd worry about getting the cage open later, but right now they felt somewhat safe, locked in the cage. The growling came closer. Paws and claws sounded on the stairs as the creature slowly came closer. The two troublemakers huddled together at the back of the cage, hoping the bars would keep the monster out.

"I hope it loses interest…" Eric whispered, trying to keep his tone light, even though he felt scared that the bars wouldn't hold and that the monster would maul them.

The monster came down the stairs and snarled as it saw its prey sitting there, ready for the taking.

It took a lot of control for both of the boys to not scream at the snarling creature.

It was a wolf, a giant freaking wolf.

The growling continued, the intelligent eyes of the beast landing on one of the guys first and then the other. When it got to the door of the cage, it stopped and stared at them.

Derek wondered if the wolf would just sit there until they opened the door or passed out? Did it like easy prey?

The wolf sat down on its haunches, keeping its eyes on them, and then the wolf moved without moving.

Sinew stretched and contracted. Fur receded. The boys stared in horror as the furry creature transformed right in front of them. Human skin became visible and intelligent eyes stared back at them.

The man stood tall outside of their cage and they stared at him, their jaws on the floor. Had that just happened? How had he done it? Who was the guy? What was that guy?

"Are you done?" The man growled. The boys huddled even closer together at the demand in his voice.

"What are you?" one boy piped up, too scared to ask with more than a whisper. The guy growled once again.

"I said, are you done?" He demanded, the tone of his voice voiding all arguments the boys might have made.

"Yes…" they both said in unison. The guy nodded and turned on his heel to walk back upstairs.

"Good. I'll let you out in the morning and then you can go around repairing all you've broken." He growled, not even sparing them a glance.

The next morning, the man had got dressed and stood in front of the cage door with a broom in one hand and a key in the other.

"Rise and shine, boys, it's time to clean." His gruff voice rose them from their sleep. They had leaned partly on each other and partly on the wall when they slept, so when Derek stood abruptly, realising where they were, Eric slid down to the hard stone floor, waking up when he landed.

The man opened the cage and held out the broom for them to take.

Derek held his hand out and took the broom, careful not to touch the werewolf's hand in the process. He didn't know if it was contagious or not. He wasn't even sure he had seen what he thought he had the night before. Eric moved out of the cage with a hand on the side of his head where he'd hit the floor. Deflated from a night in the cage, they crept up the stairs and out of the big doors. They never should have seen the open door as an invitation to go inside, even with the wolf scaring them outside.

Sighing deeply, they got to work.

Sound: Uuh uuuhh – Skull – Witch's boot – Ghost

"Uuh uuuhh…" The sound came accompanied by waving fingers, moving closer.

"Just stop!" Taylor said, annoyed that her one terrible reaction to a ghost was to be ammunition for her boyfriend to tease her mercilessly. "It's not funny anymore"

"Yes, it is. Who would have thought the big bad witch was afraid of ghosts?" He chuckled and nudged her gently with his shoulder. She knew it wasn't meant in a bad way, but it still annoyed her.

"I'm not afraid of them. It just surprised me." She tried to explain, but knew he wasn't listening to her, not really. Taylor wasn't afraid of ghosts. She really wasn't. She couldn't afford to be with her abilities.

"Right, I'd go with that explanation too if it was me who jumped several feet in the air when she saw a ghost." He chuckled again. Taylor picked up one of the couch pillows and brought it swiftly to his head to make him stop.

"Ow… so that's how you want to play it?" He raised a brow at her.

"Clearly," Taylor laughed as her boyfriend jumped on her. Making her lie flat on the couch with him on top of her. His hands found her wrists, pressing them down on the couch.

"Remember whom you're playing with…" He said ominously, but Taylor just laughed. She knew he wouldn't do anything she didn't want him to, and that he was just teasing her.

Lifting her head, she kissed him on the nose. He gritted his teeth with a glint in his eyes and gathered both her hands in one of his above her head, and then used his other hand to tickle her. She couldn't help laughing, but still tried to struggle against him.

"That'll teach you not to mess with me," He laughed, trying to keep a straight face, and failing miserably.

"Are you done yet?" The voice came from behind them, and they turned to see who had been talking. The translucent shape of the ghost hovered a few inches above the ground, staring at them both. Its hands were on its hips. It was the same ghost who had surprised her earlier.

Taylor pushed at her boyfriend to get him to let her up. She hadn't expected the ghost to talk to them, or to talk at all. It was the first time she'd heard it, and she was stunned. Her boyfriend sat up and he, too, stared at the ghost, trying to see if he'd made it up in his head. He looked at Taylor, trying to gauge if she had seen and heard the same thing he had.

"Did the ghost just talk?" He asked. Taylor just nodded.

"Really? Young people these days…" the ghost said exasperatedly, almost huffing at them. It seemed to both of them that the ghost didn't think they were good enough for it to spend its time on, but that they were the ghost's last option.

"Can't trust them to listen when their elders are talking. Back in my day…" The ghost kept talking, even though Taylor and her boyfriend had stopped listening to stare at each other. The ghost was berating them for being young and modern compared to the youth that it had apparently encountered when it had been alive.

"Excuse me… but why are you here?" Taylor asked, fearing the answer a little. It was never a good sign when ghosts showed up and it was an even worse sign when the ghost started talking. She knew it was even though no ghost had ever spoken to her before. Taylor had planned that they were going to spend the night on the couch, watching the horror films they were showing on the television. She had even made sure that no trick-or-treaters would disturb them while they were watching. Taylor had made her boyfriend put the bowl of candy outside the door with a sign that said the children could take a piece of candy each.

She knew that at some point the bowl would be empty, either because someone got greedy or because a lot of children had come by, but by then they would have watched at least one of the films they had planned on watching, and they could fill up the bowl again if needed.

"No manners…" The ghost huffed again. It started pacing on the floor, which looked comical since the ghost was floating above the floor. They didn't comment on it, though, since it would only make the ghost more agitated and they didn't need that.

"I need your help. Why else would I be here? Good-for-nothing little witch…" The ghost sneered at them. Taylor knew she shouldn't take offence to the ghost's words, but she couldn't help but feel a little offended. She might not seem all that powerful, but she was powerful enough for what she needed.

"What do you need my help with?" Taylor asked, trying to keep the growing anger from her voice. The faster she could help the ghost, the faster they could get on with their night.

"My unfinished business," the ghost stated, as if it was the most obvious thing in the world. Taylor tried not to let her annoyance show.

"What is your unfinished business?" She asked, trying hard to keep her tone light, but knowing there was an edge to her voice she couldn't quite remove. It was just her luck that their spooky date night got disrupted.

"I'm not sure I like your tone, young lady." The ghost said. The ghost reminded Taylor of her old grandmother. She'd been a prickly lady, very set in her views on the world and on people. Her demands were impossible to live up to.

"I'm sorry. I can go back to spending time with my boyfriend instead of helping you if you don't appreciate my tone…" Taylor said, this time entirely unable to keep her annoyance out. The ghost huffed again, but went quiet. Taylor raised a brow at the ghost, waiting for it to tell her what it needed her help with.

"What will it be?" Taylor asked then, getting a little impatient. She knew that the first Halloween horror films had begun on television. It was a marathon, and she'd been looking forward to watching as much of it as possible.

"Fine. I can't move on until I have finished the unfinished business." The ghost stated. Taylor didn't even comment on it. It was obvious it was what unfinished business meant.

"My best friend and mortal enemy…" The ghost started, and its words made Taylor pay attention. She knew it was getting good when the story started with a best friend and a mortal enemy.

"…have finally passed away, and I swore on my deathbed that I'd bash in her skull." The ghost said. Both Taylor and her boyfriend looked at the ghost with wide eyes. Had the ghost just said what they thought it had?

"Wait… you want me to bash in the skull of your mortal enemy because she has finally passed away?" Taylor asked. She needed clarification.

"Yes. I want you to bash in her skull before she gets buried. I can't do it myself, and it's the only thing I have left to do." The ghost said impatiently. Taylor had a hard time wrapping her head around it.

"But, why?" She couldn't help but ask.

"Because she did the same to me, except I wasn't dead at the time." The ghost tried to explain, finding its audience a tad bit slow on the uptake. They didn't have all night after all.

"Did she kill you?" The boyfriend asked, just as horrified as Taylor felt.

"Yes, now pay attention. I vowed as I laid there dying that I had to get my revenge and the only way I can do that is if you help me." The ghost grew even more translucent with the amount of power it used in its explanation.

"We don't have all night. Will you help me or not?"
The ghost asked then, trying to tap her foot on the
floor and its hands firmly planted on its hips.
"Will you leave us alone if I help you?" Taylor asked,
hoping it wouldn't take long or that the task the ghost
wanted to be done could wait until later that night or
another night.
"Yes. I can finally move on when you help me
complete the task." The ghost promised.
"Fine then. When and where?" Taylor stood up from
the couch to her boyfriend's dismay. He'd been
following along the conversation, hoping that without
his input, it would get done faster. The ghost seemed
like he was in a hurry. He knew Taylor knew what she
was doing, but agreeing to help the ghost might not
be a good idea. He grabbed hold of her arm before
she could walk away from the couch.
"Are you sure you should indulge this ghost? What it
needs doing sounds highly illegal…" He said in a low
whisper. Taylor nodded. She thought it was illegal
too, but she couldn't come up with any other options
for their problem with the ghost.
"I have to. I'll be back soon." She promised before
she went into the bedroom to change.

Standing outside the funeral home, Taylor felt like she
was about to do something illegal, and she probably
was. How the ghost had talked her into actually doing
it, she hadn't any idea.

The ghost was hovering beside her, staring through the window at the display of coffins and urns. Taylor had never loved being near dead people and she'd never ever set foot in a funeral home, either. That was about to change.

She'd changed her clothes before she'd left home, knowing that she didn't want to be spotted. She'd found a black oversized hoodie where the hood covered her face perfectly, and then she'd put on a pair of black leggings.

The weather had been fairly warm, even though it was late October, so she wasn't cold in her get-up, but she supposed that the adrenaline coursing through her veins was helping too.

"She's in there, in the back. I checked. The coffin hasn't been closed fully yet." The ghost stated, acting a little nicer now that Taylor was actually going to help.

"What do you mean it hasn't been fully closed?" Taylor tried not to stare too openly at the ghost. She didn't want to give away that something weird or paranormal was going on.

"That they haven't nailed the lid shut yet." The ghost's impatience with Taylor clearly showed through his words. They couldn't keep standing on the street like they were. They had to get moving. There weren't many people out, but there were enough that they'd get noticed sooner or later.

"Don't they do that immediately?" Taylor hadn't any idea how it all worked. She'd never been or wanted to go behind the scenes at a funeral and after this, she hoped she never would have to do that again.

"Well, they were going to until I scared them away."
Everything the ghost said made the bad feeling in the
pit of Taylor's stomach grow bigger.
"Why would you do that?" Taylor looked inside the
funeral home once again. The front of the place was
dark, and all the lights were off. It was late, and she
hoped they wouldn't have any alarms set. All of her
magical skills lay in a different area, and she couldn't
do anything about electronics and alarms, however
much she wanted to.
The ghost raised a translucent brow at Taylor as if she
should already know the reason.
"So how do we get in, or did your master plan not
include a way of entry?" Taylor asked, wishing she
was at home on the couch with her boyfriend,
watching a horror film and not living through one.
How was she talking with a ghost as if it was a real,
live person? She hadn't any idea.
"They left the back door unlocked when I scared off
the workers in there…" The ghost sounded smug and
a little proud of itself. Taylor couldn't help but feel
bad for the workers. Her own first encounter with the
ghost hadn't been the best either.
"Can you show me the way?" Taylor asked as she
moved along the side of the building, already feeling
the apprehension growing. It was perfectly legal for
her to walk on the street, but what she was about to
do definitely wasn't legal.
Taylor and the ghost got to the door. Taylor tried the
handle and found that the ghost had been speaking
the truth. The door wasn't locked, it was hardly even
closed.
She hoped they wouldn't experience other break-ins
other than hers tonight, since the door would still be

unlocked after she left. Though she didn't really know what would be in there that would be worthy of theft. Taylor opened the door and stepped inside. Closing the door behind her, she made sure it didn't lock her inside. She wanted an easy way out.

"Where are they keeping her?" Taylor asked the ghost that had just stepped through the closed door. She hadn't waited for the ghost to go through the door with her, because she hadn't thought it was necessary.

"This way…" the ghost said and floated ahead of Taylor, going down the corridor to the right room.

It was freezing when Taylor stepped through the door. There were several slaps and refrigerated doors. Taylor supposed that was what a morgue would look like. Along the opposite wall of the refrigerators was a closed coffin.

"Is it this one?" Taylor asked, trying not to let her teeth clatter in the cold. The ghost nodded.

Taylor walked to the coffin and opened the lid a little hesitantly. She hadn't any idea what was waiting for her when she opened the lid. She only knew it would be an old lady.

What met her eyes was a friendly face. The woman looked like she was sleeping soundly, and Taylor supposed she was. The second thing she saw was the necklace that the woman was wearing, and it made her close the lid and turn to look at the ghost.

"She's a witch?" Taylor asked.

"Does it matter?" The ghost said. Taylor nodded gravely. She looked around on the floor and saw the boots that had to be the woman's. Her witch's boots. Grabbing hold of the left boot, she bolted from the funeral home. The ghost followed right behind her.

"That was not what we agreed!" The ghost sputtered. Taylor kept running, taking all the back streets until she got to the nearby forest. There was no way she was going to bash the head in on a fellow witch, regardless of any wrongdoings the woman had done in her life.

Taylor only stopped when she got deep into the forest. She bent over with her hands on her knees, the boot still in her hand. She was trying to catch her breath from all the running. The ghost stopped beside her. Its arms crossed over its chest.

"This was not what we agreed! You were supposed to bash her head in, not steal her shoe!" The ghost huffed. If Taylor hadn't known already that the ghost wasn't strong enough to pick up physical things, she would have been a little frightened.

"Isn't this better? I stole one of her boots because this way she'll go into the afterlife with only one shoe on and I don't have to get arrested for mutilating a corpse of a fellow witch. The other witches would shun me," Taylor tried to explain, throwing the boot on the floor.

It was a boot similar to the ones Taylor owned herself. She only wore them when she was casting, and she knew just how important they would be to the dead witch. Important enough to make it into the casket with her.

"If you want someone to bash her head in, you'll have to find someone else to do it. Either move on and find your friend in the afterlife or leave me alone." Taylor stomped out of the forest, leaving the boot on the forest floor and the ghost flabbergasted.

Taylor didn't know why she hadn't told off the ghost before they'd left her home. She should have done it. They had wasted the entire night.

"I'm sorry… Thank you for trying to go along with my request. I'll move on." The ghost appeared right in front of Taylor, making her jump backwards in surprise. The appearance surprised Taylor so much that she hadn't heard what the ghost had said.

"What?" Taylor asked.

"I'm sorry…" the ghost said. Taylor didn't know if the ghost was being truthful or not. She supposed it didn't matter, as long as the ghost moved on soon.

"Thank you for helping. I'll move on now." The ghost added. Taylor watched as the ghost slowly dissipated and disappeared fully.

Taylor stood still, watching the place where the ghost had been. Had it really gone? She wasn't sure, and she didn't want to walk into any remnants of the ghost if there were any in the air.

Stepping around the place, she walked in a circle around the place, giving the remnants of the ghost a wide berth. She walked the rest of the way home. Hoping that her boyfriend would still be awake and that there would still be Halloween films showing on the television.

When Taylor opened the front door, the entire place was quiet. She stilled in the doorway, listening. At first, she couldn't hear anything, but then she heard her boyfriend's light snoring coming from the living room.

She walked into the living room and saw her boyfriend sleeping soundly in the soft glow of the moonlight coming through the window. She smiled, sighing softly.

The film marathon had to wait for another night, it seemed. She walked to the couch and pulled the blanket off from the back and draped it over her boyfriend and then went to bed herself.

Stary night – Spider's web – Candle – Ghost

The night sky twinkled overhead like someone had dropped a tin of glitter on it.

It was surprising, not because the stars were out, but because the weather forecast had claimed it would rain. We'd been hoping for clear skies for the moon to really stand out, and we'd been devastated when we'd heard the weatherman say it would rain on the 31st.

Like how hard was it for the weather to keep the skies clear on Halloween, especially with the full moon happening as well? The weather had to be nice, even if it would only be that one time.

I couldn't believe our luck, as it seemed like the weather had listened to our wishes.

We'd been planning for months. Waiting for the right time to try out our little plan. None of us was a witch or anything paranormal, but we wanted to be. We wanted to be paranormal bad enough that we'd go to any lengths to achieve it.

We'd been dreaming about being otherworldly since the first time we ever heard a fantasy story. For me, it was Dracula and for Sam, it was *'Cycle of the werewolf'*. It was the first thing we bonded over when we met. Instantly we got talking about the different supernatural creatures and whether we believed they really existed.

Sam had said that he absolutely believed in werewolves, vampires, the fae and witches. I was a bit more on the fence about it. I knew it was possible that they existed among us without us mere humans knowing, even knowing about the witch trials in the 1600's. It was still unclear if the women and men who was convicted of witchcraft had even been genuine witches at all. For them to have survived, they would have to blend in perfectly, making it hard to go around accusing anyone of anything.

The more we talked, the more we agreed werewolves were the coolest of the supernaturals. Sure, Dracula and the vampires had their pull, but being undead didn't appeal to any of us. The fae was a tricky bunch, and we didn't even want to get started on the research needed to even contact them. They made deals, and the deals were always in their favour, and we didn't like that.

We didn't have any powers that witches had, and we didn't know how to get any, either. No book we could get a hold of could tell us just want to do, so they were out as well. Sure, we could try demon summoning, but those always ended badly. That left the werewolves and all the myths and legends about them.

We'd read the French myth, about the Loup Garou and the other European werewolf legends in the library. They seemed the most likely species that we could turn into and not die while trying to turn or lose our souls.

So, we'd scoured the internet for information on how to turn into a werewolf. We didn't want the Loup

Garou version of a werewolf. The 101 days of the wolf wouldn't be enough for us. We wanted the freedom to change whenever we wanted.

We'd finally found a list that seemed somewhat reliable and that was why we desperately needed the October full moon to be visible. Not only was it October and a full moon, but it was also Halloween and we believed it gave the moon a little extra power that would help us become what we wanted.

Sam lived in a dorm room a little away from me. I still lived at home. He was coming over later, and when my parents had gone to bed, we'd sneak outside and then walk out to the forest.

We had found all the things we needed for the night to be a success. All we needed to do now was to perform the rituals and make sure the light of the full moon bathed us.

I smiled at the thought, thinking that after tonight, we'd be a part of the supernatural community *if it existed*. Sam was adamant that it did, and I so hoped he was right. I wanted it to be true so badly.

I heard a knock on my window, and I opened it, letting Sam climb inside. My parents couldn't know that he was coming over or that he was in my room after nightfall. They didn't trust me and him together, even though we were only friends.

"Hey, Charlie!" He greeted me with a smile as he landed softly on the floor of my room.

"Hey, Sam. Did you bring everything?" I greeted him and sat down on my bed. He nodded and pointed at the backpack I hadn't seen he was wearing on his back.

"Of course. It's too important. We can't make any mistakes tonight." He said, he kept his voice low. He

knew how my parents felt about him and about me
having a boy in my room.
"Okay. My parents will check on me before they go
to bed, which shouldn't be long now, so hide under
my desk until they've gone to bed?" I asked, hopeful
that he'd understand.
Luckily, he understood and hid under my desk. I got
down under my blanket, making sure that I'd pulled
the blanket up under my chin to hide that I was still
fully dressed.
My parents didn't knock when they checked on me.
They expected me to be asleep already and didn't
want to wake me. I both appreciated that they cared
for me that much, but it also annoyed me because I
had no warning of when they were coming. When
they'd first started checking on me, I'd had a habit of
reading and they'd scolded me for not sleeping yet.
Now I kept my eye on the time for when they would
check and then pretended to be asleep when they did.
I heard my door close quietly, and I peeked at the
door with one eye open. It was fully closed. I could
hear my parents talk on the other side of the door,
but I couldn't hear what they were talking about. It
didn't matter either. It was probably just plans for
Christmas or something like that. Halloween had
never been their thing.
I waited for ten more minutes, knowing that they'd
hear me if I got out of my bed now.
When I was sure they'd gone to bed, I almost sprung
out of my bed, making sure to not step on the
creaking floorboard. I had hidden my boots and my
warm jacket under my bed, and I hurried to put them
on.

Sam came out from under the desk and stretched his legs. We didn't speak. We didn't need to; we knew exactly what we were going to do and how we were going to do it. The first step – getting out of my house unnoticed.

We both went to the window and opened it slowly. When it was finally open wide enough for us to climb outside, we did.

The cold air was biting into my skin. Winter was definitely coming soon, even if the sky was clear, and the moon shone brightly high in the night sky.

Sam closed my window behind us just enough that it wouldn't look like it was open, but not enough that we could open it from the outside when we got back. We walked in silence. The weight of what we were about to do weighed on our minds as we walked. We didn't want anyone to notice us or ask us just what we were doing out this late.

Getting to the edge of the forest took longer than we had planned, but we still had time. Sam looked at his watch to confirm and then nodded to me. We did still have time. We walked into the forest and towards what we believed to be our destiny.

"So, how do we do this?" I asked him as we walked, breaking the silence.

"We need to find one of the paw prints and then we'll set up there," Sam said confidently, and I smiled. We were really doing this. I started looking down at the ground, looking for a paw print, but it was almost impossible to find any. The ground had frozen solid and had been for a little while.

"Can you see anything?" I asked Sam, noticing that he was walking a little away from me. We had to stick together, or we might get lost. Everyone knew a pack of wolves roamed around in the forest. At least that's what people kept saying. I'd never seen them, and neither had Sam.

"No, but Charlie, maybe we should stick together. That way, we can get started a little faster when we find a paw print." Sam called out. I hurried to get to him and together we walked further into the forest. It took several minutes before the imprints on the ground began. Apparently, October was a horrible month to do this ritual when it was cold because the ground had frozen, and wolves couldn't make paw prints on the frozen ground.

The imprints we found were shallow and didn't quite resemble a wolf's paw. I wondered what kind of animal had made them and how long they'd been there?

"Over here, Charlie!" Sam called out. He slung his bag off of his shoulders and down to the ground. He picked up the candle from his bag. We had agreed to use a candle, even though it wasn't needed. We felt like it was necessary and made it seem more like a ritual than anything else.

I walked through the underbrush to get to him, ruining more than one cobweb on my way there. I brushed off my trousers and sat down on the cold ground beside him, looking directly at the paw print he'd found.

It was perfect. It had the right shape, and there was even a little water or dew gathered in it. All we had to do now was to wear the wolf's fur Sam had got off of eBay and then drink the water from the paw print.

It was simple, and yet it grossed me out a little. Drinking water from the ground felt unnatural. I knew that historically people would have drunk from streams and any other source of water that they could, but this was modern times with modern plumbing.

"Are you ready?" Sam looked at me with the most beautiful glittering eyes I'd ever seen. They glittered more than the night sky had done earlier.

"Yes." I just said, breathlessly. He handed me the wolf's fur that he'd got for me. A beautiful silvery grey fur that had a few dark markings. I slung it over my shoulders to wear it as a cape. He pulled out his own wolf fur and slung it over his shoulders. It was a darker fur than mine, but still beautiful in the moonlight.

He looked at me and winked, then leaned down to drink directly from the paw print. Sam made sure something was left for me to drink when he got back to the sitting position. He had a little dirt on his lower lip, and I felt the urge to brush it off with my thumb, but kept my hands to myself. I hadn't any idea if doing so would disturb the ritual.

I was about to bend down when I heard it.

The wolf howl sounded far away, but at the same time, it sounded like it was right behind us. I sat up straight and looked at Sam, who had an equally horrified expression on his face. What were we supposed to do now?

"What do we do?" I mouthed to him, and he shrugged his shoulders just enough for me to see it and understand his meaning. He hadn't any idea either. What were we going to do?

The howl sounded again, and it brought the frigid chill in the air straight into my bones. We stood slowly, looking around, trying to spot the wolf, knowing that it would be a little later when we saw it.

I pointed at the way we'd come from and tried to gesture for Sam to move back in that direction. We had to sneak away. Letting the wolf's fur fall to the ground and leaving the candle, which had blown out in the wind, we edged our way out of the forest.

The howl sounded even closer this time, and the accompanying growl had the hairs on the back of my neck standing up straight. It was getting too close, clearly hunting us.

"We have to run," I heard Sam, and I didn't hesitate. I started running, with Sam right behind me. We ran as fast as we could to get out of the forest. The wolf gave chase. I could hear each time its paws hit the ground, and it was running faster than we were.

Sam screamed. I'd never heard him scream before. I turned mid-run and saw the wolf had its teeth in Sam's calf. The wolf was huge. I'd never seen a wolf of that size before.

I didn't think as I picked up the biggest branch I could find and charged back towards Sam and the wolf. I started swinging the branch in the air, hoping that it would scare the wolf away.

It didn't let go until I actually hit it on its head. Sam scrambled to his feet, having a hard time standing on the leg that the wolf had bitten into.

The wolf growled at us, and I swung the branch again, hitting it on the head again. Giving up on us, the wolf turned and ran into the underbrush again.

I let go of the branch and turned to look at Sam, who was white as a sheet. His leg was bleeding a lot, and we needed to find help somehow.

I know we'd be in trouble, and it didn't matter. All that mattered was getting the help Sam needed. I

placed his arm over my shoulders and helped him
walk out of the forest with me as support.
His injured leg couldn't support his weight, and it
took too long for us to get out of the tree line.
"Did you bring your phone?" I asked Sam. I'd
forgotten mine at home. I hadn't thought I needed it.
"Back pocket." He said, his voice strained to the
point of exhaustion.
I picked out the phone from his pocket and dialled
the emergency services. I explained what had
happened, well not all of it, but the most important
part. A walk in the forest and then the wolf attacking
us.
I helped Sam lower himself to the ground when we
reached the nearest street to wait for help to arrive.

Sam's face was a ghost of his old self. It had been
almost four weeks since the wolf attack. I could see
the pain in his eyes and just how little he'd been
eating the past week. The symptoms had landed him
in the hospital, and they all thought he might be
dying.
They were giving him fluids and tried their best to
keep their hopes up, but it was looking bleak.
The wound Sam had got from the wolf still hadn't
healed and secretly I was hoping it meant he would
turn werewolf with the coming full moon. He seemed
to get even sicker as the full moon approached.

Sam was hoping, too. I knew he was. He didn't say it,
but he was hoping the illness was just the precursor
for the lycanthropy to take effect.
I laid my hand on his arm. His arm felt hot and
clammy to the touch, and I had a hard time keeping
up the hope it would be lycanthropy taking over his
body. It scared me. He looked like he was dying.
I stood, needing to get home and pray to the God I
didn't truly believe in. It was almost always like that.
People could go around their entire lives not believing
in anything and then, when they truly needed it, they
would turn to the God they'd been told to believe in.
I didn't believe in religion, but I would believe in it
for Sam if it meant that he would pull through
whatever was plaguing him.
"Charlie…?" He rasped out. I turned to look at him
and a scream tore through my vocal cords. What met
my eyes was a horrible cross between a wolf and a
human.

Dracula – Werewolf – Bones – Coffin

The moon hung low in the sky, its fullness a welcome sight, even though Dracula couldn't see as well in the light as he could in the darkness.

He was flying high above the city, listening to the sounds below with his bat hearing. He knew that every child in town was out trick or treating. Most of those children would have one or both of their parents with them, making sure they were safe.

He'd taken part a few times before and had enjoyed it, but he didn't feel like doing so this year. The last time, he'd scared a few of the children on purpose and then their parents, who hadn't noticed who he was, had scolded him for giving their little sensitive goblins nightmares.

Some parents had become a little overprotective in recent times, and he didn't really know if that was a good thing or not. He didn't have children himself and he would never have children. That part of his life died the night he had turned into a vampire. Seeing how children were in modern times, he was thankful that he wouldn't have any, though he missed the company a partner would bring.

It got lonely sometimes, being in the big scary castle at night when the city was sleeping.

Dracula swooped down and sat on the roof of a house, looking at all the children scurrying around in their costumes. He saw several dressed as the stereotypical vampire with the high collared cape and the plastic glow-in-the-dark fangs in their mouths. He would admit, though, that it was nice not being hunted with pitchforks and torches the second the town learned about his presence.

His bat form took flight again and this time he wanted to fly over the forest. He always flew that way when he was going home. The view of the treetops, all of them in shades of orange and the lake in the distance, brought him a semblance of peace each time.

A whimper reached him from below, catching his sensitive ears and his attention. Dracula flew around in a circle, trying to find where the whimper had come from. He flew down between the leaves and the branches and landed on one of the lower branches. He looked down at the ground and saw a dog caught in a bear trap.

Those blasted humans wouldn't let the wildlife be, and now a dog had its leg trapped. Dracula couldn't help but feel annoyed at the human's ignorance. They needed to keep away from the wild animals and let them thrive. Not only that, but it could have been a child or a teenager who had stepped into the trap.

Dracula knew deep down that until a human got hurt in the trap, they wouldn't remove them.

He flew down from the branch and landed on the ground in his human form. He'd used his magic to transform mid-flight, landing fully dressed on the ground.

Going closer to the dog, he noticed just how big it was. It was pawing at the trap but was only making the wound on its hind leg even worse.

"Shh… I just want to help." Dracula said in the calmest voice he could. He didn't want the big dog to snap around and bite him. The dog seemed to understand him a little and calmed down considerably.

Dracula walked around to the trap, letting a hand run through the fur of the dog, calming it at the same time. The fur was soft, and Dracula wanted to touch more of it. He wanted to cuddle with the dog and make sure it never got hurt again. Dracula had never felt so protective of another living being before in his life.

He moved his hands slowly down the dog's hind leg, down to the trap, letting the dog know just what he was doing.

"I'm going to open the trap, but you cannot run away just yet. We need to make sure your leg isn't broken." Dracula spoke calmly, and the dog laid down its head on the ground. Dracula wasn't sure if it was because the dog had given up or just given its permission for Dracula to help it.

He took hold of either side of the trap and used his strength to pry it open. The second the trap was open enough for the dog to take out its leg, it did.

The dog didn't run, both to Dracula's surprise, but also to his relief. He wanted to bring the dog home and keep it, but first, he needed to treat it.

He threw the trap into the bushes, hearing it snap closed, rendering it unusable for the time being. No other animals would be trapped inside the trap until the hunters got back out to check them.

Dracula picked up the dog in his arms, noticing just how big the *little guy* was. He smiled. It was just what he needed. He needed a loyal friend that could keep him company. Regardless of who owned this dog, he had to keep it.

He wondered what kind of breed it was, as he started walking towards his home. It was one of the bigger ones, that was for sure. He would have to look it up when he got home, or maybe he'd have to actually visit one of the human businesses and have a vet look at it.

He decided that if the leg didn't start healing or if it had broken, he would bring the dog to the vet, otherwise, he'd take care of it himself.

Looking up at the full moon, he tried to calculate how much time he had until the sun would be up. Did he have enough time to tend to the wounds, or would he need more time?

He had no supplies for dogs at the castle, but he was sure he would figure out something or have to go shopping tomorrow night before all the shops closed. He'd have to research just what a dog ate too and find a collar for it.

Dracula almost walked into the closed door when he got home. He'd been preoccupied with making plans in his head for the dog and just how good life would be now that he had someone to keep him company. Dracula opened the door with his elbow, careful not to jostle the dog too much. He used his foot to close the door behind him.

Several rooms in the castle had stood unused for a long while and just stood empty, with white sheets over the furniture to protect it from all the dust that could accumulate over the decades.

He chose the room on the ground floor, thinking it would be easier when the dog needed to be let outside to do its business, that it didn't have to go up and down the stairs. He walked into the room and directly over to the bed, putting down the dog on the white sheet covering the bedding.

Dracula made sure the dog was comfortable on the bed before he left the room, going searching for anything he could use for a water bowl if the dog was thirsty, and a few bones it might want to chew on. He found a bowl in the kitchen and filled it with cold water.

He had to let the water run for a little while before it ran clean, not having used the sink in the kitchen for quite a while.

Going around the kitchen, he tried to find anything he could use to treat the wound on the hind leg. Any soap or bandages, even plasters, but he didn't find much.

He went around looking for anything else he could use. He found one of his own shirts when he went down into the basement, thinking that any type of cloth would be better than no bandages.

Dracula found another bowl and this one he willed with warm water. He couldn't find any soap that he thought he could use on the dog, so he left it out. Clean water would still help a lot, he thought.

Getting back to the guest room, he found the dog panting on the bed. It seemed like it had tried to sleep, but the pain in the leg had been too much and had kept it awake.

"Don't worry, little guy, I'll clean it and wrap it up so it can heal and then you can sleep up here on the bed or with me in the basement," Dracula said with a kind smile that showed the tips of his fangs.

The dog blew out a breath and once again Dracula wished he could understand what the dog was telling him. He put the bowl with the cold water on the floor beside the bed. Dracula placed the warm water bowl on the bed. If it spilt any water, it wouldn't matter all that much. He had plenty of rooms he could move the dog to if the bed got too wet.

He took the shirt and started ripping it into strips that he placed beside the bowl. Some strips were long and others were shorter. The sleeves on the shirt he just ripped off of the shirt. Those he would use to clean the wound of any dirt and bacteria he could.

"Okay, so I'm going to get this cloth wet and then I'm going to clean your wound. Please don't bite me while I do that, okay?" Dracula spoke softly as he narrated what he was going to do.

He dipped the cloth in the warm water, making sure it soaked through before he pulled it out and wrung it in his hands over the bowl. He leaned down to inspect the wound. It looked horrible. The skin looked torn in several places, because the dog had tried to get free, and in some places, the wound went all the way to the bone. Dracula winced a little before he gently started cleaning out the wound.

Dracula took great care of the wound, leaning in close to inspect the wound each time he dipped the cloth in the water to clean it a little. He checked if the bone looked broken or splintered, and luckily, it didn't. He made sure he had cleaned out all the dirt he could find. Every insignificant speck washed away.

He then left the cloth in the bowl and brought out the other sleeve. Dracula carefully arranged the torn skin

back into place as best he could before using the
sleeve to bind the wound tightly. He held on to the
sleeve and then took the fabric strips to secure the
sleeve in place.

Dracula paused and looked up, meeting the dog's
brown eyes, and smiled sympathetically at it.

"There, all done. Now, let me clean up a little. It
seems like we've made a mess of the bed." The dog
whined. Dracula hoped the dog was thanking him,
but for all, he knew the dog told him he was
incompetent that he hadn't brought it to a vet.

Dracula stood and picked up the bowl with the warm
water and the leftover fabric strips. He left the dog on
the bed as he walked back to the kitchen to rinse out
the bowl and throw out the cloth. It had once been
one of his good shirts, but he felt it had served its
purpose now.

Getting back to the room, he sat down beside the
dog, his fingers automatically finding the soft fur at
the top of the dog's head. Digging his fingers deeply
into the fur, he found he was relaxing more than he
had in a long while. He knew he'd done the right
thing for both him and the dog.

The dog whined again.

"I'm sorry, I don't understand what you're saying,
little guy…" Dracula said absentmindedly, now
thinking that he needed to find a name for the dog if
he were to keep it.

"Do you have a name little guy?" He asked, moving
his hand to scratch under the neck. The dog whined
again.

"I don't suppose you could tell me if you did. So how
about I find one for you and you can tell me if you
like one of them?" Dracula suggested as he moved to

sit on the bed with his back against the headboard. He moved the dog's head to lie on his lap, so he could continue stroking its head.

"How about Jack?" Dracula asked. The dog huffed. "Okay, not Jack then. How about Wolfie? You kind of look like a wolf mix," Dracula then suggested. The dog huffed once again, blowing out hot air on Dracula's exposed wrist.

"Okay, okay, how about Spot?" Dracula was sure that if the dog could have raised an eyebrow at him at that suggestion, it would have.

Dracula lifted his head to look out the window, finding the sky lightening slightly. Daytime was coming.

"Time is running out and I need my beauty sleep," the dog huffed again at his words. Dracula began getting up from the bed, but the dog didn't move. It kept its head on his lap. He had to edge out from under it.

"I know what you're going to say, but I didn't get to stay this pretty by staying up all day." Dracula joked. He stood from the bed, even as the dog tried to keep him in place.

"Now, do you want to stay up here and sleep, or do you want to sleep in the basement next to my coffin?" Dracula liked the thought of the dog staying with him downstairs, but he didn't know how he'd be able to let it out during the day if it needed to go to the garden.

The dog wagged its tail against the bed, and Dracula took it as a clear sign it wanted to come with him. He bent down and lifted the big dog up in his arms. He was careful of the hurt hind leg still when he started carrying the dog towards the door.

Dracula walked slowly, careful not to let the dog hit any doorways or furniture on the way to the basement door. He struggled with the door to the basement, but he didn't want to put down the dog, knowing that the floor wasn't all that soft.

"When we get down there, I have to go upstairs again and find you something to sleep on. I hope you won't hate me too much during that time." Dracula talked to the dog like it could understand him.

He finally got the door opened and started down the stairs, knowing the door would close automatically behind him.

Dracula felt it the second the moon dipped below the horizon. Not because his kind was ruled by the moon, but because the dog in his arms started changing into something else. He'd been wrong, he'd been so wrong.

The wolf in his arms grew smaller, and he had to scramble to still hold on to it and not let it fall down the stairs. He stared at the transformation. How the snout fell in on itself and turned into a human mouth and nose. The eyes changed shape, but still held the same warm, brown colour. How the body shape changed, and the fur receded into the skin again.

It only took a few seconds until he was holding the naked human woman against his chest in a bridal carry. This was not what he had expected when he'd helped the dog, when he'd still thought it was just a big dog in the woods.

"Thank you…" the woman whispered before she became slack in his arms. She'd fainted from the pain, still present in her leg. The transformation hadn't healed it.

Dracula stood gobsmacked, still holding her, not knowing what to do. How he hadn't sensed that the dog was a werewolf and not just a normal dog was beyond him. He felt a little disappointed and sad at the loss of the dog that had never been his to begin with.

Dracula walked down the stairs and laid her in his coffin. He couldn't really do anything else. Dracula went back upstairs, finding the bedding he needed to arrange a makeshift bed for her in the basement with him. He hurried back down, burning the last of the darkness, getting ready for his daytime sleep.

Dracula stared at the woman for a few moments when he'd got what he needed from upstairs and then he moved her to the bed he'd made on the floor.

He could hear her heart; it beat steadily in her chest, and it calmed him. He got into his coffin, closed the lid, and fell asleep.

Bones – Coffin – Dracula – Pumpkin

Dracula looked at his coffin. He'd gone out this evening and now there were bones on the lid of his coffin, and he didn't know where they had come from.

He knew he didn't have any visitors. He couldn't sense anyone in his home from where he stood. Dracula lived too far out of town for anyone to venture out there to prank him like this, only to leave and not stay around to see his reaction.

He looked around his crypt, trying to find all if any clues about where the prankster had gone.

Dracula had gone down to get one of the spare candles he kept in stock down there. He could see pretty well in the dark, but it was still nice to have candles lit.

It helped with the aesthetic of being the infamous Count Dracula, and he liked how they made creepy shadows wherever he placed them.

He had a reputation to uphold, and someone pranking him didn't do well for his self-esteem or his image as the scary vampire.

The bones didn't even look real. They looked like plastic skeletons that they sold for cheap at the local supermarket.

The deep sigh escaping his lungs only annoyed him even more. He wasn't supposed to let things like that get to him that much.

It wasn't the fact that someone left a skeleton on his coffin, but that someone had breached his innermost sanctum and had the gall to brag about it. This was the place that was supposed to be the most secure in the entire castle. Protecting him while he was dead to the world during the day.

He walked to the skeleton and grabbed hold of the foot, which had been dangling off the side of the coffin lid, and pulled the skeleton off of his coffin, only to drag the coffin with it.

"No!" He exclaimed as he realised just what the prankster had done. The skeleton was super-glued to his precious coffin.

"This can't be happening." The exasperation build up inside him. Dracula was over it. He was over Halloween and over humans. It could only be a human teen that had pulled a prank like that on him. They were so young and foolish and not afraid of anything, especially the new generation.

Dracula leaned down to examine just how the skeleton had been glued to his coffin and if his coffin would even be presentable after removing the blasted skeleton.

Looking closer, he saw that not only was it glued with superglue, but the culprit had glued every part of the skeleton to the coffin. He tried to pull at just a single piece, but it didn't want to give.

He had a bad feeling that he'd have to either live with the skeleton on top of his coffin or destroy the skeleton and his coffin. Afterwards, he'd have to go buy a new coffin, and how would he do that?

There were no mortuaries or funeral homes where the opening hours extended into nightfall. He didn't know if it was because they just didn't want to work that late or if they were afraid of who would come knocking when the sun went down.

Giving up on trying to get the skeleton off and deciding to deal with it later, he went to the storage room to find the candles.

What met him in the storage room wasn't the box of candles he knew should have been there. It was even supposed to be full. What met his eyes was a pumpkin carved like a vampire.

This prankster was just mocking him, wasn't he? Dracula slammed the door to the storage room. He was furious at the prankster. He didn't even know who the person was, but he was sure of one thing. They'd be dead the second he found out their identity.

Stomping up the stairs to get to the ground level of his castle, he muttered under his breath. He was planning out just how to take his revenge before killing the bastard who was ruining and moving his things.

With each step he took, he got more and more annoyed at the guy who had pranked him. He knew it just had to be a guy. Women were more refined in their pranks and less obvious, or so he'd found through the years of people-watching.

Dracula opened the door and stepped out into the hall. He hadn't noticed anything odd when he'd got home, but he'd also gone directly to his crypt when he'd come through the door, wanting to find the candles.

"Whomever you are… I'm coming for you." Dracula seethed. He figured he'd have to check every room from top to bottom, just to make sure the culprit had gone and that he hadn't done any more damage to his beloved home.

Laughter sounded from upstairs. Dracula turned around so fast that his cape flailed around him, making everything light move in the wind it created. He sent out his senses to locate the intruder while moving to the stairs quickly to get upstairs, before the person laughing left. He almost fell over his long cape.

Finally, upstairs he went from room to room, feeling something was off, but he couldn't put his finger on what it was. There was something missing or something added, but he couldn't put his finger on it.

"Where the hell are you?" He yelled at the laughter. Dracula could hear it moving, always out of his reach. He was not in the mood to chase anyone today, not when he had his coffin to fix and his candles to find. He moved as fast as he could from room to room without finding the prankster.

"I don't have time to play hide and seek with you!" He yelled at nothing. He simply couldn't see anyone. Hearing the laughter coming from upstairs this time, he hurried to the stairs to search the rooms above him. He was getting more and more annoyed at the game the prankster was playing with him.

It was the same upstairs. There was no one up there. Dracula went through each of the rooms, once again feeling like something was wrong with his décor. He just couldn't place what it was.

Dracula went slower this time, trying to figure out just what the prankster had done. He let his eyes glide over anything, but he couldn't figure out what was missing or added.

Turning around to go into the next room, he figured out just what the prankster had done. Sitting on the wall mounted candleholder was a miniature pumpkin decoration. It was no taller than two centimetres. Dracula picked the little pumpkin up in his hand.

He was going to kill that blasted prankster when he found them.

Dracula went to the next room and looked around carefully, this time finding a mini skull decoration on top of some books on his bookshelf. He picked up the little skull and put both the skull and the pumpkin in his trouser pocket.

He went around to all the rooms on the second floor and when he finished, his pockets were full of the mini decorations. Dracula was fuming. He would get the prankster to clean everything and find every little annoying decoration before Dracula killed him.

He heard the laughter again. This time from the attic. There was no way he was going up there. No, he'd prepare his revenge, a revenge that the little bastard would have to clean up afterwards, too.

Going back to the first floor, he went through all the rooms once again, this time knowing what he was searching for.

Pockets full of small Halloween decorations, he went back to the ground floor and walked to the cleaning closet. He opened it, relieved to see that the prankster hadn't removed anything or added those decorations in there.

Taking the mop bucket out of the closet, he held it in his hand as he walked back down to the basement.

He had all the important repair stuff stored down there in the colder air.

Walking to the closet, where he knew he'd find the carved pumpkin instead of his box of candles, he drew in a deep breath, steeling his nerves. He still hated that someone had been down in his most holy sanctuary.

Most of all, he wanted to close his eyes so he wouldn't see the pumpkin, but he knew that would be counterproductive. He wouldn't be able to find what he'd gone down there for if he did so.

Trying hard not to look at the pumpkin, he looked at the shelves for the tin of paint he knew he kept in there to make small repairs on his home. It wasn't as if he could just go to the paint store for fresh paint each time something needed a fresh coat, so he stocked up on it. He couldn't exactly get a repairman to come fix things at night, either.

Dracula placed the paint tin in the bucket, closed the closet door behind him, and then walked upstairs again. He then remembered that he hadn't checked the rooms on the ground floor for the decorations.

Dracula could still hear the laughter from upstairs, so he felt fairly certain that he wouldn't get interrupted during his planning. He went into his kitchen.

He had no use for a kitchen, but it was nice to have to let unsuspecting humans think that he actually ate normal food. Make them feel at ease if they ever came knocking.

He smiled at the thought of his last visitors. They'd been missionaries for their religion, and he'd let them in and served them tea. The tea had expired, but sugar had hidden that fact well.

He remembered how they had talked about their religion being the only way to save his soul from eternal damnation and how much better his life would be if he just believed in their God and all their religious teachings.

They'd talked for hours before Dracula had got bored with them. He'd used his powers on them and made them sit still while he drank from them. Blood was and would always be his only religion.

He'd given them both plasters to place on the tiny pinpricks he'd left behind and sent them on their merry way.

Placing the bucket on the kitchen counter, he emptied his pockets into the sink. He didn't like the feeling of the bulging pockets against his thighs, and he liked the decorations even less.

He wasn't against celebrating of Halloween, but he never decorated for it. It ruined his well-thought-out gothic décor.

After having emptied his pocket, he went back to the bucket. He took out the paint tin and placed it on the counter.

Dracula debated if he should mix the paint with something or if just paint would be enough… No, just paint wouldn't be enough. He went into the living room, the room where he had entertained the two religious people, and picked up one of the couch pillows.

Dracula knew there would be feathers instead of stuffing in the pillows because he had given the decorator very specific instructions when he'd redecorated.

He brought the pillow to the kitchen, placed it beside
the bucket and then went searching for a knife to cut
it open with.
The knife was very light in his hand, but sharp still.
He picked up the pillow with one hand and then held
it over the bucket.
Cutting into the fabric was easy. Getting the feathers
to land in the bucket wasn't. He emptied the
pillowcase into the bucket and gathered up as many
of the stray feathers as he could afterwards.
Satisfied with the number of feathers, he went to the
paint tin and opened it. The deep red colour was
perfect for his plans. He poured the entire tin into the
bucket.
Dracula watched while the paint slid between the
feathers and coated them nicely. He sometimes
wished he owned one of those modern cameras.
Taking a picture of the prankster covered in feathers
and paint that looked like blood would be worthy of a
picture frame in his crypt.
Smiling to himself, he hefted up the bag by the handle
and walked around downstairs to find the perfect spot
to place the bucket. He knew it needed to be
somewhere that the prankster might go through, but
it also had to be believable that the door would be
open and opening outward, so they couldn't see the
bucket before it was too late.
Deciding to place the bucket above the front door, he
went outside.
"I hope you're gone by the time I come back." He
yelled to the prankster, not sure if they could hear
him or not, but at least he gave them a fair warning.

He opened the front door loudly and then closed it behind him hard enough that he was sure it sounded throughout his entire home.

Dracula opened the door as soundlessly as he could and placed the bucket over it, balanced only by the door and the doorframe. He hoped the prankster would go out through the front door, otherwise he wouldn't get to catch him.

Dracula walked down the front steps and into his garden, looking for the perfect hiding spot, where the culprit wouldn't spot him from the door and where Dracula could see the front door clearly.

He sat down behind a bush, looking through the leaves. He didn't know how long he would have to wait, but he'd wait right until the sun was about to rise if he had to.

It didn't take long before the prankster showed up. He was looking around to both sides, holding on to the door handle as he slowly pushed the door open. Dracula kept his eye on the bucket. It wouldn't be long now before it would fall down and cover the bastard in paint and feathers.

The door creaked a little as the prankster looked around the yard as they pushed the door open. Dracula's smile grew as the bucket fall in what seemed like slow motion. Logically, Dracula knew that it all happened quite fast, but his perception of time changed for just a few seconds as the bucket fell down.

It turned around in the air and as the bucket landed right over the prankster's head, the paint and the feathers started coating him.

Dracula couldn't help but laugh loudly when the bucket landed on the prankster. He stepped out from behind the bush and walked up the stairs to his front door and the pain in his behind.

"Now, that will teach you not to play a prank on me ever again." He said in a gleeful tone. The prankster used his hands to lift the bucket off of his head and then let it fall to the floor.

"You are going to right all the things that you've done to my home and you're going to clean off the paint from my front steps," Dracula demanded. The prankster lowered his head, clearly and properly defeated.

Bones – Witch's boot – Ghost – Stary night

The race against the sun had begun the second Luna had closed down the shop.

The last customer had taken their sweet time finishing with their purchase, and usually, Luna didn't mind all that much, but this time she was on the clock and the clock was running faster than Luna wanted it to.

The customer finally left, satisfied with her purchase of herbs and crystals. Luna usually tried to guess what the customers were trying to do, and she usually took the time needed to give the customers the advice they needed. This time she hardly looked at what the customer had put in their basket or thought about the uses. She'd just rung it up and kindly sent the customer on her way.

Luna had got her bag and gardening tools ready at lunch and put them by the back door so she could lock up and then take the bag and go directly to the forest behind the shop.

She'd chosen that spot for her shop specifically. Not for the customer flow, but for the forest behind it. She knew the forest by heart now, and she knew exactly where some herbs were growing.

Luna grabbed her bag quickly as soon as she had locked the front door. She hurried out the back door and fumbled a little with the key before she could turn the lock. Throwing her keys in her pocket, she hurried down the path, going behind her store, leading into the green foliage. She had to hurry, so she almost started running. The race against the sun - an actual thing.

She knew the way to the plants she needed to gather, and first, she needed more lavender. She'd found lavender almost everywhere in the forest. The iconic purple flowers stood out for anyone to see. In reality, she couldn't have easily grown it in her own garden, but since she'd found it in the wild, she knew their magical properties could be stronger.

Luna was also running out of catnip, of all things. She knew that a lot of her customers were cat owners and that it had a variety of magical uses, but it still surprised her that so many people had bought it lately, so she had run out of it.

If she looked at all the herbs she was running out of, she could easily start thinking that her customers were the most stressed people in the town and that they wanted to relieve it.

The catnip was found at the edge of a clearing further into the forest. She knew that most of the other herbs were in or around that area as well. She hadn't harvested from there in a while, so she hoped she could harvest a lot, so she didn't have to buy the fresh ones from other sellers or have bought the dry stuff. It was nearing winter, and she wouldn't be able to harvest any as soon as the first snow fell.

She knew it was late in the year to harvest, being Halloween and all, but it was her last chance and she hoped that there would be plenty still available when she got there.

When she'd found the sage plant, the first time she'd
been in the forest. She'd been more than thrilled. She
knew that the wild one would be best for magical uses
and that if she'd planted it herself, the effects would
diminish, if at all positive for the use her customers
would use it for.
She knew that if one needed a sage plant in their own
garden, they'd have to have someone else plant it.
Luna wasn't sure why, she just lived by it. The plant
wasn't native to her place, but someone else had
planted it and she was thankful for it.
She needed sage as well, both for herself, but also for
her customers, who had emptied her supplies.
The honeysuckle she needed, she knew, she might not
find, and that would be fine. It wasn't a plant that
could be found in many places in the forest or in her
area. She'd gather it if she found it, but she didn't
have her hopes up for it.
The lemon balm grew almost everywhere, especially
in the full sun. It's seeds usually spread the plant and
spread it wide. It was an invasive plant and Luna
usually did what she could to contain it, but with her
shop, she hadn't had time to come out and remove
the seeds from the flowers before they'd blow
everywhere.
Luna felt her boot hit something hard, but moveable.
It brought her out of her mental planning of how to
go about gathering the herbs and made her stumble,
making her fall to the ground.
She'd dropped her bag off of her shoulder when she
fell. She sat up on the ground, checking for wounds.
Luckily, the forest floor had given her a softer landing
than the hard asphalt would have done. She hadn't
bruised, but only got dirt stains.

She gathered her bag up and stood. It was lucky that she hadn't dropped anything from her bag that she'd have to spend her time gathering back into the bag. Looking behind her to see what had caused her to fall, thinking it was one of the bigger rocks, she saw something she hadn't wanted to see ever.

It was the skeleton of the size of a child.

Luna took a step back in horror, almost dropping her bag from her hand. How did the body of a child get into her forest and how long had it been there?

The bones were clean, but Luna knew it would take several years, if not longer, to happen, and yet she hadn't come across the body before. She always walked on this path, so the only explanation could be that one of the wild animals had got to the remains and cleaned off the bones.

Sorrow hit Luna hard in the chest. She felt deeply for the poor child, having ended their life in such a brutal way. Luna hadn't any idea if it was a boy or a girl, but she knew, with the grief she was feeling, she had to do something, even if it was only to make sure that the child had moved on.

Luna moved closer to examine the bones of the child. The child hadn't been older than six years old when they had been killed. Luna couldn't imagine what could make a person want to kill a child this size or let them wander into a forest for them to get killed.

Luna hadn't heard of any children being missing or that any police had been searching for anyone because parents couldn't find their children. It had been a fairly quiet year on that front.

Either the child had been there for quite a while and animals had moved the child within the past month or the murderer had placed in the forest recently.

Touching the bones hesitantly, she wanted to know if there would be any emotional residue left on the bones. If the death had been horror-filled, the essence of the emotions would still be present in the bones, if the death had been recent.

Luna closed her eyes and concentrated on her own magical gift. She knew she didn't work in a profession that would help her hone her skills as an empath and yet. She found that customer service jobs demanded quite a lot of patience and empathy, especially if the customer was mean. Luna could talk reason to them, affecting their emotions with her ability to calm anyone.

The gift flared to life inside of her and the horror the poor child had felt during their last moments in life hit her like a freight train. The death hadn't been quick, and it had been painful. She had to know who this child was. She had to either find the parents and give them the horrible news or find the person responsible for putting the child there.

Either way, she wasn't gathering any herbs today.

Luna opened her eyes to her second sight and found the ghost of a malnourished little girl. The ghost was looking down at what Luna assumed would be their bones. The sadness etched into the ghost's face was one she never hoped to see on a child ever again.

"Hello… who might you be?" Luna asked gently, not wanting to scare away the ghost before she could get her answers and maybe send the ghost where she needed to go in the afterlife.

The ghost girl turned her head and looked at Luna. Surprise clear on her face. Luna smiled kindly.

"Can you talk?" Luna asked. The ghost shook her head and mouthed the word no.

"Do you understand me?" She then asked, and the ghost nodded.

"Did you die out here?" Luna had to know what kind of perpetrator she was going to look for. The ghost shook her head.

"Okay, did you die at home?" Luna would ask about a lot of other places until she'd narrowed the place down if the ghost shook her head again, but to Luna's surprise and horror, the ghost nodded.

"Were you killed?" Luna could feel the hesitation and the sorrow deep in her body. She didn't want to know, not truly, but she needed to know if she were to help the little girl. The ghost nodded again.

Luna had to take a second to compose herself and calmly ask more questions. She couldn't storm off to the girl's home when she didn't know where it was, but the rage filling her body, knowing the girl had been killed, was hard to contain.

"Was it a stranger who killed you?" The ghost shook her head.

"Was it someone in your family?" The ghost nodded, sadness colouring her features.

"Did you live with them?" The ghost nodded again. Luna felt the knot of rage inside her body grow even more. She had a bad feeling about the situation, and now it made sense why she'd felt such urgency to get into the forest. The fates had meant for her to find and help the girl get justice.

"Was it one of your siblings?" The ghost shook her head.

"Was it one of your parents?" The ghost nodded. The knot of rage inside her grew even more. How could a parent do such a thing to their child? Luna hadn't asked how the girl had died and she didn't want to know either. She just wanted to bring the murderer to justice.

"Was it your mother?" The ghost shook her head, sadness colouring her features and darkening her eyes.

"So, it was your father?" Luna asked, already feeling bad that she was making the ghost go through the trauma of remembering their own murder. The ghost nodded, closing her eyes.

"Do you want me to help you cross over?" Luna had to think about something else. She'd always learned that everything you would send out in the universe would come back to you, and she really wanted to curse the little girl's father. She just didn't wish a similar curse to fall on herself.

The ghost hesitated a little before nodding.

"Do you want me to make sure your father gets what he deserves?" Luna asked, and the ghost didn't even wait for Luna to finish speaking before she nodded. Luna sighed and sat back on the ground, needing a few seconds to think of the best way to do it. She'd have to figure out who the guy was, first, and then she'd have to place some sort of spell or curse on him, so he could get what was due. She just didn't know how to do it. The ghost girl just stood watching her, waiting for something to happen.

"Can you show me where you lived?" Luna asked kindly. If she was to do anything about it, she'd have to figure out who it was. She couldn't cast a spell big enough to hit all the men in the town. Not only didn't she have enough power, but it would also cause a lot of unnecessary chaos.

The ghost pointed away from the direction Luna had come from. Luna just gestured for the ghost to move in front of her so she could follow behind. Luna stood and made sure her bag was on her securely. The ghost started moving, with Luna following. They got to the edge of the forest and the ghost seemed to shimmer, even though Luna still had her second sight up. She hoped the ghost could hold until they got to her house, otherwise Luna wouldn't know whom she needed to have arrested for murdering his own daughter.

The ghost kept walking, leading Luna from the dirt path in the forest to the sidewalk of a residential street. The longer they walked, the more see-through the little girl got.

Luna could barely see the girl when they stopped in front of a house that had seen better days. The front yard had overgrown to the point there was no path leading to the door or any driveway at all.

"Did you live here?" Luna asked quietly, hoping there would be no one else around to hear her talk to a ghost they couldn't see. A lot of the town already thought she was a weird one with her herbs and crystal store. The girl nodded.

Closing her eyes and holding out her hands with her palms towards the house, she started whispering. She was praying to the goddess that the man inside would get what he deserved, and that the little girl would find peace. She repeated her prayer, vowing that if nothing happened within a few days, she'd come back and make sure it would.

Luna turned towards the ghost and smiled kindly.

"We need to wait for the universe to do its thing. Do you want me to help you move on now?" Luna tried to be as kind as possible towards the ghost, but it was hard. The girl shook her head from side to side. She

didn't want to move on. Luna winced. A ghost
unwilling to move on could end up being a problem.
"Do you want to see him brought to justice first?"
Luna then asked, understanding why, if that was the
case. The girl nodded.
"Okay, come find me when you're ready, then." With
another kind smile, Luna turned on her heel to go
back to her home.
She lived on top of the store, and she felt a kind of
lucky in that regard. She didn't have to live with an
abusive parent or go through neglect as the little girl
had.
A few days passed. Luna hadn't been able to leave
work and go out to the forest to gather the herbs. She
wasn't sure if it would be a good place to gather until
they solved the little girl's murder. She'd have to wait
and then go out and magically clean the place of bad
intentions.
The bell above the door rang and a couple of women
came in. Luna knew both of them as closet witches,
living in one of those residential areas. They were the
type of people who practised their craft in secret,
behind closed doors. Where the neighbours wouldn't
have any idea what was going on next door.
"Esme, did you hear about the Taylor house?" One
of them asked the other. They were walking around
along the shelves, just browsing if they needed
anything.
"Oh, gosh yes. Such a horrible tragedy! He was such a
nice man, wasn't he?" Esme answered and picked up
a bundle of dried sage. Luna couldn't help but listen,
feeling like they were about to gain valuable
information. Usually, she wouldn't eavesdrop, but

something in her told her she needed to do it this time.

"He wasn't though. Did you see it in the newspaper? They're saying he killed his own daughter." Charlotte said, horror filling her voice.

"No, that can't be! The little girl was an absolute angel. How could he have killed her?" Esme's hand shot up in front of her mouth as she gasped.

"She was such an angel, yes. Did you hear her mother died earlier this year from illness?" Charlotte said. Luna couldn't help but feel even more sorry for the little girl, having lost both her parents abruptly like that. One lost to illness and the other to neglect. In Luna's opinion, the little girl's father had lost it when he started neglecting the little girl.

"Yes, yes. An absolute tragedy for that family." Esme agreed. "So how did they figure out that he'd killed their little girl?" she then asked, having not read the newspaper as Charlotte had.

"Apparently, his firm suspected he was embezzling from the company, so the police showed up with a search warrant. They searched the entire house and found her room and at first, they asked him where the girl was. He lied and said she was with an aunt. They didn't quite believe him, I think, so they phoned the aunt and she said she hadn't seen the girl in months, so now they were treating the girl as a missing person and had interrogated him for hours before he cracked and told them what he'd done and where he'd put her." Charlotte had read more than the newspaper. She had a friend at the police station, and it might have been illegal for her friend to share, but she still had, finding the crime just as horrible as Charlotte had.

Luna couldn't help but think something had answered her prayer, but at the same time, she felt so sorry for the little girl that her own blood-kin had killed her.

"Have they asked him why he did it?" Esme had to ask. They had stopped browsing and were just engulfed in the story that Charlotte was telling.

"My friend said that he had just told the police that the girl had been annoying and one day he'd just snapped," Charlotte answered. She didn't know how the little girl had died, no one really knew, and the police hadn't released a statement on that part yet.

"Oh, it's just horrible, is what it is!" Esme said and turned to the shelves again, remembering that they were in a store and that they both needed stuff for their craft.

Luna stopped listening, feeling a presence off to the side. She turned her head towards it. She didn't see anything at first, so she used her second sight instead. Luna saw the little girl. She was glowing brighter than she had before.

"Are you ready to go?" Luna whispered gently. The little ghost nodded. Luna smiled.

"Do you see a light?" She asked, and the ghost nodded again.

"Go into it, it's safe," Luna whispered, and the girl turned around, looking at something Luna couldn't see. The ghost started walking and gradually disappeared until she was gone.

Luna straightened with a gentle smile on her lips. Tomorrow she'd go into the forest and purify the place so the herbs would be usable next year. Tonight, she'd just relax and order the herbs she hadn't gathered. She was just happy she had got to bring balance and justice to the world again.

Candle – Demon – coffin – Witch's hat

The fires of hell…

That was how hot the kitchen was as the demon appeared in front of the stunned witch. "What did you do?" The demon's voice cut through the sound of the smoke alarm going off and the witch stopped frantically trying to disperse the smoke by waving her witchy hat under the smoke alarm.

"I don't know…" The witch coughed and tried frantically to get the smoke to stop. The demon looked around the small kitchen, trying to find the source of the smoke and the heat. His eyes fell on the soup pot on the stovetop. It was smoking more than he'd ever seen hell do. He walked to it, free to move, since the summoning hadn't happened inside a circle. He looked inside the pot, finding it completely black and charred. Whatever she'd been cooking in the pot had died twice and gone to hell, and it had taken the pot with it.

"Clearly…" the demon commented and then went to the window to open it for her. He wasn't there to help, but he found that generally, the summoner was easier to talk to when they weren't dying from smoke inhalation, though it would be easier to steal their souls when they were close to death to begin with.

It took a little while, but finally, the smoke disappeared. The demon had taken the entire pot and put it outside. Removing the source of the smoke, ad taking the worst of it with the pot. The witch lived in a house in the woods, and since there was no fire in the pot, only smoke, he thought it would be safe enough to place it outside.

He turned to look at the witch, who just stood there, dumbfounded.

"What are you…?" She asked, "Who are you…?" her mouth almost gaping at the sight of him with his wings and hellish appearance. Runa had been too busy with the smoke and waving her witchy hat around to comprehend that someone had talked to her. She had thought it was one of her friends coming by at a terrible time. She had been wrong.

"I'm Nymgarraman, servant of the infernal king Bilet," the demon introduced himself with a bow. He was trying a different tactic this time, not wanting to fail for the second time. No need to tell her just what he did for a living. He needed a witch to join him in hell and she would be as good as any. He'd truly wanted the other witch he'd tried to take, but he'd gone about it all wrong and had suffered banishment for his troubles.

"But you, little witch, can call me Nym." He added, knowing his full name was quite the mouthful for the mortal tongue.

"Nym, right… So, what are you doing here?" She asked him, not even knowing how he'd got there. Demons weren't supposed to just pop up on earth without being summoned, and she was absolutely sure she hadn't summoned him.

"I believe that this…" He gestured around him at the entire kitchen. "Had something to do with me being here. Though I'm not sure it was intentional. Just what were you doing, little witch?" He asked, a bit of wonder colouring his voice.

"I… I was just cooking dinner and then forgot about it…" she said, hanging her head. She was a mess in the kitchen and had always been. She never did potions because they always turned out wrong. This time she'd wanted to cook food for the first time, thinking that if the pot was big enough that it wouldn't go wrong. Then she'd left the stew to simmer and gone to read the new book she'd got. She'd got lost in the book until the sound of the smoke alarm had gone off.

"I'm sorry to inform you it's not quite the way to cook dinner." He chuckled and leaned his hip against the counter, looking at her.

"I know, I know. I'm just dreadful in a kitchen. I mean, you're here. It can't very well get any worse." She sunk down in a chair, not even worrying about the demon that was free in her kitchen. If the demon wanted to, it could go out into the world and wreak as much havoc as it wanted, and no one could stop it unless they could catch him in a circle. And that wasn't easily done.

"I dare say. I've never tried a summoning by failed cooking before. That, I must say, is a first." He chuckled again.

"I'm glad my misfortune brings you joy." She said with a wry smile. He chuckled once again and smiled at her. The sight of his smile made a shiver run down her spine. He looked menacing when he smiled. She didn't know if it was because of his teeth, being sharp and pointy, or if it was the fact that a demon smiling never bode well for anyone.

"Now, we've taken care of the trouble with the pot, and I assume you're not dying right now from the smoke, yes?" He asked and crossed his arms over his chest, making his biceps bulge a little.

"I'm not dying as far as I know." She said, hoping that she could make the demon leave soon. It was dangerous to have a demon run loose in the world.

"Oh good, now, since you brought me here, I suppose I have to ask what it is you wish from me?" Nym asked, pushing away from the counter to walk closer to the little witch. He was curious about what she could come up with. He had to trick her into making a deal with him. A deal that would make him able to bring her to his realm. To bring her back to hell with him.

"I… I've never summoned a demon before. What do people usually summon you guys for?" She hadn't any idea what to even ask from him and what she'd have to give for it in return. There were tales of demons being the bad guys all-through history.

"Oh, this or that…" Nym said noncommittally.

"No, really. I haven't any idea why anyone would summon a demon, let alone how…" She didn't like that he wasn't answering her questions like she wanted him to. She didn't even know what kind of demon he was or what he could do for her, if he could do anything.

"Yes, well, it doesn't get done much, so being a demon is kind of boring, to be honest…" Nym said, making sure he was staying close enough to the truth that she couldn't accuse him of lying. The more he could seem like a good guy given a bad lot in life, the higher the chances of a successful deal being made, even if he had to lie by omission. Luckily, she hadn't trapped him in a circle, so even if she'd summoned him by accident, he wasn't obligated to tell her the full truth.

"Why do people usually summon you, not demons in general, but you specifically?" She asked.

"What is your name, little witch? I feel that I'm at a disadvantage here since you know my name, but I don't know yours…" the demon said silkily. He moved away from the counter, his movements fluid. He walked closer to the table where she was sitting.

"I'll tell you when you answer my question." She said. He smiled at that.

"You have yourself a deal, little witch." He said with a crooked smile. Runa froze at the word 'deal'. She hadn't been careful enough, and he'd tricked her.

"People usually summon me when they need to cause someone else harm. They summon me because I can make limbs tremble…" He let his words drift off, making her guess his meaning. She blushed but remained quiet.

"Now, your end of the bargain must be upheld, little witch. We can't have you break our little deal, now, can we?" His voice was seductive, making her want to break the deal more than she'd ever wanted in her life, regardless of the consequences of that action.

"My name is…" She stopped and looked at a point behind him. He turned to watch and heard her chair fall to the ground as he was looking away. He tsked at her. Nym had expected her to fight him, but that the chase would be this delicious as an extra treat. Licking his lips, he stood and followed her.

"Now little witch, running was a dangerous idea…"
He called out after her. The door still swung on its
hinges as she had run out the door in a hurry.
He walked after her, enjoying the cool night air on his
skin as he followed her. She didn't know it, but since
making that insignificant deal with him, he'd know
exactly where to find her, regardless of where she
went.
Runa ran for her life. She hadn't any idea what else to
do. She ran through the underbrush of her home,
happy that she'd spent several hours in the forest
every day since she moved out there. Runa knew
every nook and cranny and knew the exact route to
get to the rest of civilisation, but she also knew what
routes to take where she could hide out of view.
She chose the latter, knowing that she'd need to hide
and need to hide well. Runa ran as if her life
depended on it, and it did. She'd made a deal with a
demon. It had seemed insignificant when she had
made it. A name in return for information she'd
wanted, even though she hadn't wanted to make a
deal to begin with.
The searing pain just over her hipbone had been
unexpected. The minute he'd given her what she'd
wanted, and it had been her turn to make good on the
deal, she hadn't wanted to, and it was like the universe
had known.
The pain had come at that second, like a brand,
searing into her flesh. She didn't know anything about
demonology, but she knew it couldn't mean anything
good.
Runa kept running, trying not to think of the pain still
radiating out from her hip. She knew there were caves
nearby that she could hide in. The most obvious place

for her to hide would be inside one of the bigger caves, but she knew there was a crawlspace hidden behind the bushes that would make an even better hiding spot.

She looked behind her as she ran, and she couldn't see the demon anywhere. It didn't mean he wasn't following her, but it meant that she might still have a chance at finding a hiding place without him spotting her.

Crouching down by the crawlspace, she slowly inched her way inside. The last time she'd tried, she'd been younger, or the crawlspace had been bigger. It was difficult to make sure that she had covered herself completely in the space and behind the bushes.

She waited and listened. The forest was silent, completely silent. No birds were chirping, not even the night-time ones. There were no sounds of crickets either, which there usually were, this close to the lake. It was as if the forest held its breath, waiting to see if she would get out of the predicament she'd placed herself in.

Suddenly, something ripped the bush out of the ground and before she got to push further into the crawlspace, something took hold of her ankle and pulled her out. She closed her eyes, not wanting to see if the demon was angry at her for running or if it looked even scarier than it had in her kitchen.

"Now, little witch, you broke our deal…" Nym whispered, his voice snaking around her, making her feel even more trapped in his hold. He held her upside down as the hangman tarot card depicted. She wondered briefly if she could have avoided the entire mess if she'd only done her cards today.

"I… I didn't…" She tried. She was having a hard time concentrating as the blood rushed to her head, making her nauseous and dizzy.

"Oh, but you did. All you had to do was tell me your name and now your life is forfeit to me." He purred at her. Nym swung her around and hefted her over his shoulder. He didn't tell her that her life had been his to claim from the moment they had made the deal.

She kept her eyes closed, mourning her choices. What bad things could have happened if she'd told him her name? She wouldn't have had to tell him her entire name. There was power in a name, and she didn't want to hand him that power, though she supposed she'd given him worse now.

Her entire life was in his hands.

"What if I tell you my name now?" She offered, not knowing if that would work or not. He kept walking with her over his shoulder, his muscular arm across her thighs to keep her in place.

"I suppose it would be nice to know your name, spoken by those soft lips, little witch, but alas, it is too late." He sighed, but it didn't seem genuine. She got the sense that he'd got just what he wanted out of the deal and at a very low cost.

"You intended to break the deal, even as you made the deal." He chuckled. "It would seem that you were more than willing to face the consequences of your actions." He added.

He walked through the door to her home and began rummaging through her kitchen, looking for what he needed to open a portal back to hell.

Nym found a black candle in a drawer and pulled it out. He set it on the counter and then began looking for a piece of chalk. He found a piece beside the stove. His little witch was a messy one.

Nym still held her over his shoulder, and she struggled against him as he looked through her things. Nym didn't need anything more than the candle and the chalk.

He took the candle from the table and held it in the same hand as the chalk. He then pushed the table out of the way to clear the space.

Nym bent down, still holding on to her legs, keeping Runa over his shoulder, and drew a circle with the chalk. He put the chalk away on the nearest flat surface and then used a fingernail to prick a hole in his pointer finger. The blood dripped from his finger and hit the chalk circle. The entire circle turned blood-red instantly. He had put down the candle on the floor before he began drawing. He put her down in the middle of the circle.

"Now don't move." He said, and she found herself unable to do anything other than what he told her to. He didn't say a word to her while he drew, but he chanted in a language she hadn't heard before. She hadn't any idea what he was saying or what runes he was drawing inside the circle, but she knew she was in trouble.

He stood as he finished his intricate circle. He inspected his work, and apparently satisfied, he hummed. Nym bent down to pick up the candle. He lit the wick with his fingers and then looked down at her.

"Now you get to try what only very few people have tried before you. You get to go to hell without dying." He mused. His demon buddies would be so jealous that he'd got a human to follow him back to hell.

"I do promise, though, that even though you could be considered undead, I won't have you sleep in a coffin." He chuckled, and a chill ran down her spine. This was bad and getting worse by the minute.
He lifted the lit candle to his lips and spoke a few words in his demon language, and then, with a mischievous smile, he blew out the candle.
At first, nothing happened and then a sucking sensation seemed to start from her hip, wanting to pull her through the floor. Nym stepped into the circle and picked her up, and then everything went black.

12

The smell of death was all that met the Alpha's nose as he tried to find the scent of the missing werewolf.

There was blood in the air and the full moon hung high in the sky, lighting their way. The entire pack was out searching. They'd been searching for the she-wolf for quite some time, not even knowing when she'd got lost from the rest of the pack when they'd been running.

They didn't have a long time to search for her, either. The moon might be high in the sky, but it would still only be a few hours before they would have to give up their search. Humans had a habit of going running in the early morning hours and the pack couldn't risk being seen in their wolf forms.

She was important to them. She didn't know it and she hadn't been told yet, but since she'd come of age, the Alpha had been planning to court her and make her the queen of their pack. He'd had his eye on her for a while now. He'd just needed his wolf to subdue her for long enough to make his intentions clear to her.

The pack had been lucky this year. They usually did a pack run during the full moon closest to Halloween, where the Alpha, if he wasn't mated, would make his intentions known to the female he wanted, and this year they'd been lucky that the full moon fell on Halloween.

The run had started perfectly. They had run from the pack-keep. It had been their starting point, and everyone had been yipping and howling for the first few miles.

As midnight approached, the Alpha started looking for the wolf with the brown eyes but hadn't been able to see her anywhere.

He didn't think much of it at first, because there were many wolves in the pack, but as the hours dragged on, he got worried that he still hadn't spotted her.

He howled, a signal for her to respond to him, but he heard nothing. The rest of the pack howled in unison, but her voice was missing from the group. As the Alpha, he could differentiate between the voices even as they joined in a harmonious song.

The smell of death hit his sensitive nose for the second time. There were no carcasses nearby that he knew of, and he knew smells could travel, but then the smell wouldn't be permeating the air as it was in this area.

A slight hint of blood hit his nose. It was below the scent of death, hidden almost well enough that it seemed intentional. The Alpha put his nose to the ground and sniffed.

The scent was hers, mixed with the metallic smell of blood. He couldn't sense just how long it had been there, but she had definitely been there.

The Alpha growled low in his throat. He didn't like what the smell of blood implied. If someone had hurt his mate, there'd be hell to pay.

It wasn't usual that anyone ever went into the forest
and especially not during Halloween. Each and every
child would be dressed up and out trick or treating, or
they'd already be in their beds, their stomachs hurting
from all the candy they'd eaten during the night.
He knew deep down that it couldn't have been any of
the humans. If she'd been shot, he would have heard
her whine and he could have heard the shot going off.
Not a lot of things could kill them. Their fur was
thick, so it was rare that they ever got scratches from
branches and other things in the forest.
Nose still to the ground, he tried to find the source of
the blood. He searched in circles, his wolf getting
more and more antsy, the stronger the smell of blood
got.
He got to the bushes. The smell coming from inside
it. His hackles raised as he slowly got closer. He didn't
like the thought that popped through his head that
he'd find her mutilated body there. The smell of
blood was strong, but it was only the smell of blood
that was strong, not her particular scent.
Using his snout to move some of the foliage away to
give him a better view of what had hid beneath. He
felt something sticky on his nose as he rummaged
through the bush. Drawing his head back to use his
paw to remove the stickiness, he realised what he'd
stumbled into. A spider's web.
He struggled with his paws to get the web off of his
nose. Hoping that none of the pack would show up
before he had gotten rid of it. He could just imagine
how much they'd tease him back at the pack keep. He
sneezed and tried to get the rest of the spider's web
off.

The Alpha inched closer to the bush again, this time a little more carefully. He didn't need more of those sticky threads on his face. He pushed the leaves and branches aside and saw what had led him there.

The bear trap had sprung, and it had definitely caught something or rather someone in it when it sprung around its victim. There was blood around the sharp teeth, and he was certain that it was hers. His little rose was in trouble.

The Alpha howled, calling the entire pack to him. They had a pack mate to find, and they had to do it fast. Time was running out, if she'd been taken by anyone. They needed to find out where she was.

The wolves streamed in from all around him, coming from all directions to help their pack mate. Everyone counted, and everyone was important. It was no wolf left to fend for themselves, but a group that helped each other all the time.

A few of them whined at the smell of her blood. The Alpha communicated mentally to his pack, telling them about what he'd found and what they were going to do next. It wouldn't be long before the full moon disappeared, so they'd be back into human form.

They hadn't been able to find her in the forest, which led to the horrifying option of her being spotted or taken by someone.

The wolves dispersed, having got their orders. There was nothing left to do where he was.

The next step would be to check her home for her, but he'd have to wait until the moon went down. He couldn't go to her house in wolf form. Her neighbours would call animal control if they spotted a wolf out in the open, that close to the general population.

Standing on the steps outside her apartment, the Alpha knew she couldn't be home. He still walked up to the back door and knocked. He waited, wanting to try contacting her by the way of the pack, but he also wanted to show he could be patient. She might have figured out that he had planned to chase her, and it could have scared her a little. She might even have planted the bear trap to lead him off of her trail.

It wasn't every day that the Alpha chose a mate, and he knew he could seem a little scary because of his size.

A cat ran from a bush, streaking across the yard in the back of the building. She was one of the lucky ones to have the back door leading directly outside, not having to go through a hallway first.

It was the reason she'd chosen the place. The Alpha knew because the backyard led directly to the forest, and she could go there directly if a shift was imminent.

It wasn't often that happened. Each of the wolves in the pack knew when the full moon was about to hit, but having the option to go out in the forest quickly was still good.

He knocked on the door again and when she still didn't answer. He pulled out the key ring where he had keys to everyone's house. The Alpha searched through the bundle of keys, trying to find hers when one neighbour stuck their head out of the window of their own apartment.

"She isn't home. She didn't come home last night." The woman yelled, making the Alpha wince. He'd been so focused on listening for his future mate that he'd amped up his hearing.

"Thank you, ma'am. Have you heard anything about where she'd be?" He asked, deciding to be nice to gain as much information as he could from the woman.

"No clue. She's always keeping to herself. Probably out with her boyfriend or something. A young girl like her must have a boyfriend." The woman didn't give the Alpha a chance to reply before she went back inside her apartment and closed her window again. The Alpha stepped back from the door. NO, she couldn't have a boyfriend. She was his chosen mate, so there was no choice for her. She couldn't have a boyfriend he hadn't approved of.

To keep their secret safe, the pack wasn't allowed to date around, and they weren't allowed to date humans. The risk was too great, especially around the full moon.

His hand tightened around the keys, anger colouring his vision. His rational side knew he needed to find her, to ask her the reason she'd been missing. The rational part of him also knew that she might lie wounded somewhere, where she couldn't get home. The wolf in him wanted blood. It wanted to kill the boyfriend that the Alpha wasn't even sure existed. The Alpha put the keys back into his pocket and had a last look in her window, noting where everything was, so that he could notice if anything was different. He saw her warm winter coat on a coat hanger through the window in the door. He noted just where everything was that he could see from the outside. They would have to keep a guard on her apartment, to see if anyone comes looking or if she comes back. He made a mental note to put up a schedule for his pack to watch the place.

His wolf was pacing again. It wanted to try contacting her through the bond. That if they could find the tiny invisible thread that tied her to them, then they'd know she was alive.

He nodded to himself. Yes, they'd try that and then set up someone to watch her place, even if there was no thread to follow in his head.

He walked into the forest, and he kept walking until he was sure that no one could see him from the houses.

The Alpha sat down on the cold ground and closed his eyes. Using the connection to nature as a booster while he searched for his little Rose in his head.

He came up empty. He tried more than once to find even a small sliver of a thread, but there was nothing. Each and everyone else in the pack was there, but she was missing.

The roar of frustration that burst out from him and his wolf almost shook the forest.

Several days passed with no one seeing or hearing from her. The Alpha didn't want to admit defeat. He did not want to think of her as dead or presumed dead. They'd searched every inch of the forest and other places where someone could have tossed her body. They'd found nothing.

It was as if she'd disappeared off of the face of the earth and he didn't like the sound of that. She was his mate. They might not have joined, and he might not have claimed her on the run, but she was his. In his wolf's mind, she was.

Sighing deeply, he sent out the call. They couldn't go on like this. The call was to gather everyone for their mourning ceremony.

If she came back, she'd be welcomed with open arms, but with no thread tying her to the pack she had to be presumed dead, even if they hadn't found her body.

The pack gathered outside, and the Alpha stood. He didn't say a word as he joined them outside. Each one of them held a candle in their hands. Someone handed him a candle and a box of matches. He didn't say a word as he struck a match against the igniter.

The Alpha lit the white candle in his hand. He didn't want to believe that she could be gone. He couldn't find her through the pack bond, and she was nowhere to be found. There had been no ransom calls or anything to show that she was still alive.

Mrs Rose walked up to him and used the flame on his candle to light her own, the tears streaming down her face. She'd lost her only daughter, and she'd been devastated at the news. The Alpha could feel her pain through the bond, and it hit him hard.

The pain a mother felt when she lost a child was unbearable and almost brought him to his knees.

Next in line was his Beta. The wolf who had taken the place instead of Mr Rose, who had been Beta until he died a year ago. The new Beta lit his candle through

Mrs Rose's candle and that way the rest of the candles were lit, each member of the pack taking part in the grief so the burden for one person wouldn't be as great.

Last time they'd done this mourning ceremony had been when the Beta had died. The Alpha worried about Mrs Rose's mental health. Having lost two members of her closest family within a year had to be hard. Not only her own flesh and blood, her daughter, but also the love of her life, her mate.

The circle closed on the other side of him, telling him the last candle had been lit. They'd gathered outside on the day of the dead to mourn her.

Everything went silent. The Alpha bowed his head. He felt it through their bond, all of their grief and their mourning. There was no room for his own doubts that she was still alive somewhere or any room for his own grief at losing the one his wolf had chosen as a mate.

The wolf inside him howled mournfully in his head. Its melody was a sad soundtrack to the ritual. The outside world was still quiet, but the wolf inside him made his ears ring.

The pack stood like that for several minutes, no one wanting to blow out the candle and let go of the girl. They were all waiting for the Alpha to make that move first. They were all looking at him and at Mrs Rose. Neither of them wanted to say goodbye.

A slight breeze blew through the clearing, blowing out the candles. It was the universe's way of telling them it was enough.

The Alpha couldn't stop thinking about his little
Rose, his would-be mate, taken from him too early.
The thought of her occupied his mind at all hours of
the day. He couldn't just forget her brown eyes and
how they sparkled when she laughed. The sound of
her laughter and her warm presence.
It had been the reason his wolf had chosen her to
begin with. The wolf inside him paced. He had to do
something. It wasn't like him to just sit there and do
nothing.
The Alpha had to go with Mrs Rose to clear out the
apartment, but he didn't want to. He wanted to hold
on to the thought that she was somewhere out there,
still alive. Clearing out her apartment would
definitively tell them she was gone.
They didn't have to do it yet. They could wait and see
if she would return, but he also knew that the lack of
pack bond told him everything he needed to know on
the matter.
He stood, determined now. He walked to the door,
got his key from the hook, walked out to his car, and
got in.
The ride to the apartment building was a blur. He
hadn't told Mrs Rose that he was going, or anyone
else. He'd just left.
The wolf found her key on the giant keyring and let
himself inside. Her scent instantly assaulted him and it
made him take a step back. It had been a bad idea to

go there. Grief clouding his mind, mingling with the regret for what could have been.

He tried to breathe through it, dragging even more of her scent into his lungs. It took him a little while before he could walk further than the entrance.

When his mind was a little clearer, he started looking around the room. Finding everything where he knew they'd be. He'd been there before, and she wasn't one to mess things up. He looked up at her coat hangers, noticing something weird.

Her winter coat was missing. He'd been able to see the coat through the door when he'd been there looking for her. So how was it gone now?

There were no signs of a break-in, and who would break in just to take a winter coat?

Spider – Coffin – Bones – Pumpkin – Castle – Cat

"Come on!"

"No! I will not be wearing that!"

Chelsey wanted to dig her own grave over the thought of wearing the thing Hannah was holding up. Saying that Chelsey didn't like the option was putting it mildly.

"Don't be a spoilsport. It's not that bad," Hannah said, trying to convince her best friend that the costume she'd chosen would be the best idea Hannah had ever had.

"But it is, though, and you know it." Chelsey wore more fabric as underwear than what the costume was constructed of. How they could call that thing a costume was beyond her.

"It's just a nurse costume. I can't see why that's a big deal?" Hannah held up the white bra with the red medical cross over where the nipples would be.

"You're not the one who's going to wear it. It's so skimpy everyone is going to be looking at me at the party!" Chelsey was absolutely sure that her best friend was playing a prank on her. It couldn't be anything else, especially looking at the costume Hannah was holding up.

"Of course they will, and they should." Hannah's goal in life, now that they'd both turned 18, was to find boyfriends for both of them. The best way she had heard of would be to go to parties and strike up conversations with guys. The Halloween party was just the perfect excuse to wear something provocative to catch their attention.

"I don't want them to. Can't I just go as a ghost?" Chelsey wanted to hide. She'd let Hannah talk her into going, and she hadn't any idea why. Parties had never been an interest of hers. She'd rather stay home and watch films or read books. They were opposites in that regard, and Chelsey knew it.

"No! It's nurse costume or cat woman!" Hannah stated, and Chelsey sighed loudly. There was no arguing with Hannah when she was like this.

"Halle Berry or Michelle Pfeiffer's?" Those two were the only actresses Chelsey could remember having played Cat Woman, and they were also the only two Cat Woman outfits she could remember what looked like.

"Halle Berry's of course. The other one covers too much skin!" Hannah said it like it was obvious, and Chelsey supposed it really was. She knew what Hannah was like, after all.

"Just because it's Halloween doesn't mean we have to show as much skin as possible!" Chelsey knew she was right on this, but she also knew that Hannah was of a different opinion.

"Of course it does. Now, what will it be, sexy nurse or sexy Cat woman?" It was an impossible choice Hannah had given her. Absolutely impossible.

"Neither. I'll just stay home…" Chelsey knew it was unfair to threaten her with staying home, but if Hannah wanted her to go, then she'd have to accept the costume that Chelsey wanted to wear.

"No, don't ruin it for me. I want to go so bad, and my mum said I couldn't unless you were going too!" Hannah begged. It was her big chance to get a boyfriend. Who knew when the next party would be and if her parents would allow her to go to the next one?

"You know how I feel about my body. It's a ghost costume or I won't be going." Chelsey had never liked the way she looked, and had always just dressed comfortably, using clothing as a shield.

"Fine, then I'll just go dressed as Cat Woman." Hannah conceded. She figured that if Chelsey didn't find herself a boyfriend at the party, then maybe the guy that Hannah would find would have a best friend or a brother for Chelsey to date. Hannah dreamed of going on double dates with Chelsey and she'd do everything to make it happen.

"Okay then. Now, can we get ready? The party starts in an hour, so that means we have an hour and a half to get ready…" Hannah continued. She was getting a little impatient, but not enough that she'd get there early. They had to arrive fashionably late.

"Wait, are we going to arrive late?" Chelsey asked. It wasn't exactly good manners to arrive late, and she'd always been taught good manners.

"Yes!! That's what all the cool people do. That way we'll arrive when the party is going on and not when it's awkward and nobody has had any alcohol." Hannah reasoned, and Chelsey raised a brow at her.

"Don't you think they've started drinking already?" It would make sense that those who wanted to drink at the party had already started. That was the rumours she'd heard from other parties.

"You're right. We should too!" Hannah was too excited to let anything stop her from having the best time at the party and snatching herself a fantastic boyfriend, and if she needed to drink alcohol before they showed up to do that, then she'd drink alcohol before they showed up.

"No, I'm not allowed. Besides, someone has to drive us there and home again." Chelsey had never found the thought of drinking alcohol appealing. It was a way to forget troubles and get rid of inhibitions, and she didn't want to let loose like that. She liked her control and to remember what had happened the night before.

"There you go again, ruining the mood. Just one won't hurt…" Hannah pleaded, turning her puppy-dog eyes on Chelsey. Though she knew neither the eyes nor the quivering lower lip would sway her best friend, she had to try.

"You know how wrong that is, right?" Chelsey said. Hannah met Chelsey's raised eyebrow with confusion.

"What do you mean?" Hannah didn't understand. How was it wrong to want to have a good time with one's best friend?

"You're trying to get the designated driver drunk when she doesn't want to and isn't allowed to." Chelsey admonished.

"Oh… I'm sorry… I didn't think. I just really want this party to go well. It's the first party they have allowed us to go to, where they will serve alcohol." Hannah realised her mistake. She hadn't meant it like that, and she hadn't wanted it to come out like that, but it had.

"I know, doesn't mean I want to drink, though," Chelsey stated. She turned towards the mirror in her

room and stared at her reflection. She didn't need any
make-up if she was going as a ghost, did she?
"I know, I know… Now, let's just get ready, okay?"
Hannah hoped Chelsey had forgiven her. She didn't
want Chelsey to be mad. She just wanted to have fun
at the party, even if it meant that her best friend
would be stone-cold sober the entire time.
"Yes. Now, do you want to cut the eyes in the sheet
or should I?" Chelsey held up the white sheet in one
hand and a pair of scissors in the other hand for
Hannah to take. Chelsey couldn't wear the sheet and
cut out the eyes at the same time.

The music was loud enough to be heard a mile away
and when Chelsey and Hannah parked the car,
Chelsey was happy that she'd decided on the ghost
costume.
The air was chilly and even though the beat of the
music was loud enough that it felt like their hearts
wanted to beat in sync with it, the chill tore through
their costumes and into their bones.
Chelsey looked around at the entrance to the venue.
The organisers had decorated it perfectly for a
Halloween party. There were pumpkins with carved
heads on hay bales just beside the entrance, really
setting the mood of the party.
The venue itself looked like a haunted castle, and it
probably was. Chelsey didn't know how they had got
permission to throw a party there, but at the moment
she didn't care. If the police showed up to stop it,
they'd just have to flee… she hoped.

A giant plastic spider hung right over the giant doors. Hannah looked at the venue in awe and with a bit of fear.

"We should go in, right?" Hannah asked. Chelsey didn't know what it was, but something about Hannah's voice told her that Hannah wasn't sure it was a good idea. Chelsey thought about it for a second. She had a bad feeling in her gut about the party.

"We should…" Chelsey hesitated. Hannah took her hand in hers, to bring them both a bit of bravery. Attending their first party was a little nerve-wracking for them.

They walked towards the door. It was closed, but when they got closer, the doors opened seemingly by themselves. Chelsey really didn't want to go any further. She wasn't a scaredy-cat or anything, but this party might have been a little too well thought out. Walking through the doors and into the flashing lights, Chelsey had to check behind the door to see if any mechanisms had opened the door or if someone had got the job of opening the doors in a scary way. Finding nothing behind the door scared her a little. Hannah was looking around at the people. Everyone was wearing costumes, and she'd given up on trying to find any duplicate costumes. Everyone's costumes were different, because no add on was the same. One guy had glued plastic bones to a black bodysuit, which looked a little cooler than Chelsey wanted to admit. She was happy that she'd chosen to wear the sheet as a ghost and not something skimpy. It was easier to hide her slight discomfort at being there when she was under a sheet.

Hannah pulled at Chelsey's hand, wanting to go further into the room.

"Let's get something to drink," Hannah yelled. Chelsey wasn't sure she heard her correctly, but she just nodded. It was hard to hear anything over the loud music.

Hannah led them into the crowd and into the warm embrace of the music. The beat was pumping through her bloodstream, slowly loosening up her nerves and her body. She swayed to the beat and finding herself drifting away from Chelsey and into the crowd. Caught up in the moment and in the music.

"Hannah?!" Chelsey called and tried to follow Hannah into the crowd, but all the black masks and costumes made it almost impossible to find the one Cat Woman-wearing girl.

Stepping off to the side and out of the crowd, Chelsey kept her eyes on the crowd, trying to find out where her best friend had gone when the crowd had swallowed her up in all the costumes and people.

"First time?" A male voice asked, speaking straight into her ear. She hadn't seen him walk up to her or felt him beside her.

"Yes. Is it that obvious?" Chelsey asked. She had a good look at the guy standing beside her.

"Maybe a little…" He leaned in and talked directly into her ear through the ghost costume once again. She supposed he had to for her to hear him, but he had seemed to hear her just fine when she was speaking.

"I'm looking for my friend. We got separated in the crowd… Have you seen anyone dressed as Cat Woman?" Chelsey asked. The guy was taller than her and might spot the cat's ears on top of Hannah's head better than Chelsey could.

"I can't say that have, but I can help you look for her?" He offered and held out a hand for her to take. She hesitated, but in the end I accepted the help.

"I'd like that. Thank you." Chelsey was relieved that she wouldn't have to search for her friend alone, even though she wasn't quite comfortable with the strange guy.

"So, what's your name, little ghost?" He asked casually, not speaking into her ear anymore. She could still hear him, which was weird to her. She was walking behind him through the crowd. His hand securely held onto hers.

"It's Chelsey," she said. She wanted to ask about his name, but something was telling her gut that the guy was bad news. The gut feeling grew into a knot that sat heavily inside her.

"Okay Chelsey, I like the name." He continued the casual conversation. She noticed a coffin in a corner, propped up against the wall and standing open. Red satin lining almost like blood in the flashing lights.

"My name is Vladimir." He introduced himself while his back was to her. They'd got through the crowd, and she still hadn't seen her best friend anywhere. Where could she be and why didn't Vladimir have an accent? The name sounded Slavic.

Chelsey shook her head at herself. No, she shouldn't judge a guy by his name or his lack of accent. Who knew? He could have easily grown up right here in town and therefore not have an accent. She had to stop thinking about things like that.

She felt something against her legs that made her look down. Why was there a black cat at a party with very loud music? *Weren't they scared away by the noise?*

"Have you seen my friend?" Chelsey asked, but Vladimir didn't stop. He kept a hold of her hand and dragged her along away from the crowds. Had Hannah gone this way? No, she still had to be back with the crowd. She wouldn't have left without finding Chelsey. She had to believe that.

Chelsey tried to dig in her feet to stop Vladimir from dragging her along with him.

"Stop. Where are we going?" Chelsey tried to ask, but she wasn't sure if he'd heard her or purposefully ignored her questions.

Vladimir opened the door with a key, finally stopping. Chelsey tried to get him to let go of her hand while he was fumbling with the key one-handed.

"Let go of me!" Chelsey said through gritted teeth, as she used her other hand to get him to let go with his hand.

He looked over his shoulder at her.

"Didn't you want to find your friend?" He asked as if going through a locked door would help her find Hannah better than searching the crowd.

"Don't worry, I won't hurt you, little ghost. I'll help you find her. I promised." Vladimir's smile made a chill run down Chelsey's spine. Had she seen a hint of a fang when he smiled?

She was being foolish again. Just because his name was Vladimir, and he was a mysterious stranger with fangs, didn't mean he was a vampire. It could all just be an act and a costume. It was a Halloween party, after all.

Vladimir finally got the door open, and he pulled her with him inside, closing the door behind them.

At first, Chelsey couldn't see anything. The flashing lights were gone and no sources of light anywhere. Where was he taking her?

She felt him pull on her hand. She had to follow as long as she couldn't get him to let her go. His grip on her hand was like iron.

"Watch your step." He said. She stumped her foot against the first step of the stairs. She couldn't see them, and he hadn't warned her in time.

"I can't see anything in here…" she said. She felt her heart racing in her chest. Where was he taking her? She knew for a fact that Hannah couldn't be in here. He'd used a key to get in there and Hannah didn't have that one.

"We can remedy that." He chuckled. He didn't give her a chance to react before he'd lifted her up in his arms, holding her like a groom would hold his wife. Vladimir carried her up the stairs, walking slowly, as if every step held a deeper meaning than it did.

They got to another door. This one wasn't locked, only closed. He opened it, still holding her in his arms.

They walked out onto a balcony overlooking the entire party. He let her down to her feet and caged her in with his arms on either side of her.

She turned to look at the crowd, trying to locate her best friend. It was easier said than done.

"Are you ready?" Vladimir whispered against her ear, through the white sheet still acting like her costume.

"Ready for what?" Chelsey asked, still trying to find Hannah in the crowd. There were too many people down there with black masks and the flashing lights didn't really reach the edge of the dancefloor.

"Oh, just for the party to start" Vladimir moved one of his hands to her costume, pulling at the sheet slowly. She felt him pull at it and turned in his arms, noticing just how close he was standing to her.

"You should turn around and watch. You won't want to miss this, little ghost." He almost purred, looking directly into her eyes, spellbinding her, before pulling the sheet off fully, ruffling her hair at the same time. She turned as he had asked her to and looked at the dancefloor. The party was going well. What did he mean that the party was about to start? It was already going?

She was about to try turning around again to ask him when she heard the first screams. What was happening?

Pandemonium broke out on the dancefloor as several men in capes descended on the dancefloor, attacking all the partygoers.

"It's customary for the king to choose his bride first and then let the others loose on the rest. Don't worry, little ghost…" Vladimir whispered against her hair, bringing her attention back to him. He moved closer, pressing his front against her back.

He leaned his head closer to her neck and gently kissed the soft skin. She gasped.

"I have to go help them…" she sobbed.

"It's too late now, but it will be okay, my little ghost." He whispered against her skin right before she felt the needle-sharp fangs pierce her skin.

She screamed, but no one heard her. Everybody else was screaming along with her, drowning out her screams.

Everything went black.

Chelsey shot up in her bed. She looked at the alarm
clock on the nightstand. It was midnight and
November 1st had arrived. She was home and in her
bed.
Chelsey looked down at herself. The last thing she
remember was Vladimir biting her and then she'd
blacked out. She gently touched her neck with her
fingers but found the skin smooth and nothing was
aching.
Had it all been a dream, or maybe just a nightmare?
Chelsey found her phone to check if Hannah had
written to her or if she had any clues to what had
happened.
She found the text thread she had with Hannah and
scrolled through it, but there were no mentions of a
Halloween party. When she looked closely, the last
message was more than a week old.
That couldn't be right. She got out of bed, noticing
she was in her pyjamas, but had no recollection of
putting them on. She hurried to the bathroom to look
at herself in the mirror.
Something wasn't right and before she'd seen herself
in a mirror, she wouldn't be able to go back to sleep.
She turned on the lights in the bathroom and walked
to the sink. When she locked eyes with what was
supposed to be her reflection, she screamed.
There was no reflection.

Bonus

(This should be read after the story in Chapter 8 if you haven't read that one yet – go back)
Coffin – Christmas tree – Ghost – Mittens – Castle – Christmas hat

Shutting the lid to the coffin, Dracula walked up the stairs to the ground floor. He hadn't dreamt anything during the day, he never did, but he had this strange feeling in his bones that something was about to happen.

He didn't notice anything out of the ordinary when he opened the door to the hallway and he didn't see anything weird when he walked through the house, that is - until he got to the kitchen.

Ava, the werewolf he'd helped save, stood behind the kitchen island. She held a bowl of something brown in one hand and a spoon in the other hand.

"What are you making this time?" The words were out of Dracula's mouth before he could stop them. He still hadn't got used to her being in his house full time.

"Oh, good night. Did you sleep well?" Ava asked with a bright smile, looking up from her baking. "I'm baking Christmas cookies for the Christmas party." She said. She put the bowl down on the table and found flour in the cupboard. Dracula didn't know he had flour. He didn't eat after all.

"What Christmas party?" He asked, already suspecting that Ava had planned a party without telling him, only telling him because he had caught her baking for it. They hadn't known each other for very long, but he wasn't even surprised that she was planning parties without consulting him.

"Now don't be like the Scrooge. The ghost of the Christmas past, present and future will just show up and you'll realise at the last minute what a great idea this is." Ava said with a wide smile. She sprinkled flour on the countertop and let the dough spill out on the flour-covered counter.

Dracula hadn't been able to tell the woman that she needed to go home since he saved her almost two months ago. He hadn't wanted to. He hadn't before let anyone sleep in the crypt with him before, let alone let anyone touch his coffin in all the time he'd been alive. It was his sacred space and sanctuary.

"But is a Christmas party really such a great idea? I'm Count Dracula for crying out loud. I'm supposed to be scary and not someone who celebrates Christmas." Dracula sat down on the stool by the table in the kitchen. He could just imagine how people would react to him. No one would be frightened of him anymore.

"Don't be silly. Everybody in town would love to come by for a Christmas party up here at the castle." Ava argued and found the rolling pin in one of the kitchen cabinets.

Ava walked with a slight limp. Her ankle hadn't healed properly yet since she'd been stuck in the bear trap as a wolf, unable to shift back until the moon went down. Dracula had come by and been her knight in shining armour. She didn't know how to repay him for saving her life the way he had. She also felt a little guilty that he had wanted to keep her as a wolf, thinking that she was just a normal animal. How he hadn't sensed her human nature underneath her fur, she hadn't any idea.

Oddly enough, she found she wanted to stay with him, to make sure that he wasn't as lonely as she had got the feeling he was. She'd left every morning after he'd gone to bed and then come back in the evening before the sun went down, to make him think she hadn't left. She couldn't bear the thought of telling him the truth.

"I don't think people know what they're signing up for…" Dracula said as he eyed the dough on the counter. Just what was she making?

"I'm sure they'll be fine up here. You might even make more new friends." She added. She put flour on the rolling pin and started rolling out the dough. It went down easily enough.

"I highly doubt it'll be any more than a curiosity at seeing where the famous Count Dracula lives…" Dracula said, his expression turning a little sour. He liked the thought of friends, but most of all, he just wanted Ava's company.

"I'm sure they'll surprise you." She smiled as she continued to roll out the dough until it had reached the thickness that she'd wanted them to be. She went to the drawer and pulled out cookie cutters that Dracula knew he didn't own.

"Just what are you making, little wolf?" Ava's cheeks blushed as he called her little wolf. When he'd got over the first shock of her not being a male dog, he'd started calling her 'little wolf', even as her werewolf form was massive.

"Gingerbread cookies." She said, trying to hide her reddened cheeks from his sight. He didn't need to see the effect he had on her. She didn't want their friendship to turn weird.

"Gingerbread cookies?" Dracula had heard about gingerbread houses, but never the cookies, but going by the smell of them, the cookies had enough sugar to give anyone cavities, and he suspected he might have trouble calming Ava down when it was time to go to bed. He smiled at the thought of a hyperactive Ava. She started cutting out the cookies one by one, making some in the shape of a heart and others in the shape of a bell. There were a few shaped like stars too. After cutting out all the cookies, she found a baking sheet with a piece of parchment paper and then transferred the cookies to the baking sheet. She had formed the leftover dough into a ball, and she started rolling it out, repeating the process until there was only a bit of dough left. Dracula had been watching her in silence, letting her work while he came up with a plan that would stop the Christmas Party from happening.

"I have an idea…" He said, knowing it would spark her attention. She looked up at him as she loaded the cookies into the warm oven. He hadn't even known that the oven worked, and he stared at it with furrowed brows.

"Dracula…?" Ava asked, walking to him to get his attention. He hadn't heard her answer him before, being caught up in thinking about how he had a working oven. He'd never had a reason to test out the kitchen other than the refrigerator for his blood supply.

"Yes?" He said, shaking his head to come back to the present.

"You said you had an idea…? What is your idea?"
Ava asked with a smile that had a weird fluttering
happening near his heart region.
"Ah yes. Yes, I have an idea…" He said, trying to
think of what the idea was again. Ava was doing weird
things to him he hadn't noticed before. He'd thought
that it was only because he was lonely, but the feelings
persisted inside his chest.
"Yes…?" she asked, trying to make him get to the
point faster. He cleared his throat.
"Yes. I'm thinking that we could go out and I could
show you how much I'm not a Scrooge or a Grinch,
and then we could cancel the party." He suggested,
hoping she'd take the bait.
"And if I'm not convinced by the end of it?" She
asked. She wondered what he would have planned.
Ava wanted to agree to the idea, if only because it
could be fun and that they'd have a great time. She
could always say she wasn't convinced and then still
invite people.
"If I don't convince you that the old Dracula here
isn't inhabited by the Christmas spirit, I'll let you plan
the Christmas Party." Dracula was confident that he
could get her to change her mind about the party. He
didn't need people. He needed Ava.
"Okay, then." She said, wiping her hands on the
apron she was wearing. He hadn't even noticed the
apron before. She held out her hand for him to shake.
He took her hand in a firm grip, sealing the deal
they'd just made.
"Okay. Now, meet me outside in 10 minutes. If you
don't have a coat or warm boots, then I think there'll
be some in the hall closet you can borrow." Dracula

said, turning on his heel to go to his crypt. He needed to change into something he had never worn before. Dracula didn't know why he owned normal clothes, but at one point he had wanted to blend in a little, just to see what the humans did when they weren't scared of his presence. He found the warmest sweater he had. Dracula had hidden it in a chest at the bottom of his closet. He found a pair of black trousers too, a pair made of a wool mix.

He didn't quite feel the cold, but he knew that to blend in, he needed to wear the right clothes. If he didn't wear a warm coat during winter, people had a tendency to look at him funny. He didn't like it when people looked at him funny.

He found his most inconspicuous cloak, a black one, to complete the look of tall, dark, and handsome, or at least he would be, in his opinion.

Satisfied with his looks, he walked up the stairs to find Ava standing by the hall closet, wearing a mix of colours he hadn't ever seen in the hall closet before. "Where'd you find those?" He asked, knowing there would only be dark colours in the hall closet. Ava worried the colourful mittens between her fingers.

"I might have gone home to get them. You don't really have food in the kitchen, so I had to get some necessities…" She hoped he wouldn't be mad at her she'd left. He looked a little surprised.

"Oh, I didn't think of that… I'm sorry…" He said, feeling like a poor host that he hadn't thought of her needs like that.

"Are you ready to go?" He then asked, wanting to get the date started. He hadn't told her it was a date, but if he was honest with himself, he wanted it to be a date.

"Wait, what about the cookies?" Ava asked, alarm in her voice. She'd almost forgotten that she'd put the cookies in the oven and that the oven was still turned on.

"Aren't they done? Just take from out and put them on the counter to cool?" Dracula was a little unsure if that was what you had to do with the cookies, but it was what he imagined needed to be done.

Ava put the mittens in the pocket of her green coat as she walked to the kitchen to check on the cookies. Dracula stayed where he was, waiting patiently for her to come back. He heard a lot of noise coming from the kitchen before she came walking back to him.

"There. They were done, and I put them on the counter." She placed his hand on his arm, taking a chance at the closeness. He didn't remove her hand. "I'm ready to go now." She said with a smile, and he smiled back at her.

They walked outside and made sure the door closed behind them. It was getting cold outside, and Ava made Dracula stop so she could put on the mittens. She reached into the other pocket and pulled out a striped Christmas hat and put it on.

She placed her hand on his arm once again, and they started walking. Dracula was just enjoying the closeness he felt with Ava. He didn't want to break the silence, so he just led her down the path from his castle to the city.

"So, where are we going?" Ava broke the silence right as they reached one of the first houses inside the city lines.

"It'll be a surprise, little wolf." Dracula had noticed how she blushed lately when he called her little wolf, and it made him want to call her the nickname more.

"I like surprises." She didn't really need all the layers she was wearing, but she was happy she had put them on. Ava tried to hide her lower face in the coat collar so he couldn't see her blush. She knew he knew the cold wouldn't affect her as it would a normal human. They walked through the city until they reached the town square.

They had decorated the town square with baubles and lights all around it. People had sey up different booths around the edge of the square and the middle of the square had been filled with several Christmas trees.

"What are we doing here?" Ava asked, lights twinkling in her eyes as she took it all in. She knew it had been there, but she hadn't seen the Christmas market at night before. Whatever they were going to do now, she knew she'd be thankful for him just bringing her there.

"I was thinking we could get a Christmas tree. Just a small one for the two of us…" Dracula said. The joy on her face made the entire walk to the market worth it for him, even being out among the humans.

"… and decorations for the tree as well?" Ava asked, hopeful. Dracula nodded, keeping his eye on her facial expression, committing them to memory. If she left him after Christmas was over, then he'd always have this memory to treasure and keep him company, even if she'd be leaving him with a hole in his chest.

"Where do you want to start first?" Dracula asked, leaving it up to her to decide just what they would get. If she decided they needed a Christmas tree for every room in the castle, he would probably agree and buy them for her, if it meant seeing her face light up the way it just did.

"I want to find the tree first. Then we'll know how many decorations to get…" Ava suggested, looking towards the trees in the middle, her fingers itching to find the perfect tree for them. Their first Christmas tree in what she hoped would be a long line of Christmases together.

Dragging Dracula along with her, she walked to the middle of the square and soon Christmas trees in different shapes and sizes surrounded them.

"Do you see any you like, little wolf?" He whispered the endearment under his breath, to not alert the surrounding people to their true natures, but he just couldn't help himself.

"No… Where should we put it? I need to know just how tall it can be…" she mused, looking around at the different trees.

"We can put it in the living room?" Dracula suggested, wanting to hold her close to him, but he resisted. He needed to keep it friendly. He didn't want to lose her, but he also found that he wanted more than just her friendship.

"Can we really?" Ava's joy overshadowed any thoughts that went through Dracula's mind. If she asked, she'd get it. He just nodded with a smile.

Ava walked between the trees until she stood before one of the bigger ones and pointed up at it.

"This one." She said. Dracula just smiled and nodded his okay. They found the guy in charge of selling the trees and bought the tree. Since it was so big, they couldn't carry it. They arranged for the man to deliver it the next evening.

With a joyful laugh, she took Dracula's hand and dragged him to the different booths, looking at all the decorations.

At one booth, selling Christmas wreaths and candles, Dracula sensed something above his head.

Looking up, Dracula noticed the evergreen leaves with the little white berries attached to the stem. There was a red ribbon tied to it, holding the mistletoe branch attached above their heads. He knew Christmas came with mistletoe, and he knew the tradition of having to kiss the person standing with you under the mistletoe.

Ava looked up when she saw him looking up and noticed too.

"We'll have to kiss… It's tradition…" she said, a little hesitantly, biting her lower lip. She wanted the kiss, Dracula realised to his surprise.

"Well, we have to do it if it's tradition." Keeping up the charade of needing to fulfil the tradition instead of admitting that he truly wanted to kiss her.

Dracula leaned down towards her, a crooked smile on his lips.

"Last time to back down…" He whispered to her, but she just lifted her head, running the tip of her tongue along her bottom lip, showing him just how much she wanted to do it.

He leaned down further, meeting her lips in a gentle kiss. He felt her lips move against his and it spurred him on. His hands went to both sides of her head to keep her in place. He couldn't have her ending the kiss before he finished tasting her.

Ava tilted her head in his hands to get a better angle, and her hands went to his chest, not to push him away, but to grab hold of the black shirt he was wearing.

The kiss turned heated.

"Oi, get a room…" someone yelled with a laugh and Dracula reluctantly tore his lips from hers, leaving her lips a little swollen and her breath a little ragged.

"That was…" He said, having a hard time finding the words.

"…Perfect…" she finished for him with a blinding smile he knew would make him melt if they hadn't been in public.

"Yes… perfect…" Dracula knew that even though it had been their first kiss, it wouldn't be their last.